Even Villains Have Interns

LIANA BROOKS

OTHER WORKS

HEROES AND VILLAINS

Even Villains Fall In Love
Even Villains Go To The Movies
Even Villains Have Interns
Even Villains Play The Hero (books 1 – 3 omnibus)
The Polar Terror

TIME AND SHADOWS MYSTERIES

The Day Before
Convergence Point
Decoherence

FLEET OF MALIK

Bodies In Motion
Change of Momentum
For Every Action (forthcoming)

ALL I WANT FOR CHRISTMAS

All I Want For Christmas Is A Werewolf
All I Want For Christmas Is A Reaper

SHORTER WORKS

Darkness and Good
Fey Lights
Prime Sensations

Find other works by the author at www.lianabrooks.com.

EVEN VILLAINS HAVE INTERNS

LIANA BROOKS

AUSTRALIA

Trade Paperback ISBN: 978-1-925825-95-4
Case Laminate Hardcover: 978-1-922434-74-6
eBook ISBN: 9781513089874

www.inkprintpress.com

National Library of Australia Cataloguing-in-Publication Data
Brooks, Liana 1982—
Even Villains Have Interns
232 p.
ISBN: 978-1-925825-95-4
Inkprint Press, Canberra, Australia
1. Fiction—Superheroes 2. Fiction—Romance—Science Fiction

Summary: Dr. Charm's favourite daughter Delilah must team up with
the Spirit of Chicago to solve a crime mystery that will have
implications for superheroes—and super villains—everywhere.

Second Edition: July 2015
Cover Artist: Victoria Miller
Editor: Jayne Wolf

This is for the everyday heroes who save the world one day at a time.

CHAPTER ONE

December 2033

Dear Dad,

Just because Mom mentioned she liked Claude Monet's 'Grand Canal' painting does not mean she wants a copy of it for the house. I know it doesn't mean she wants the original. And telling me not to steal the piece while it's on tour at the Art Institute here in Chicago is not going to convince me to pick it up in time for Christmas. Reverse psychology stopped working when I was twelve.

In other news, you will be happy to learn that Peter Manigault, as painted by Allen Ramsay, mysteriously appeared at the Art Institute this weekend. The curator was very surprised. Personally, I think his shock was more over the two-dollar price tag left on the picture frame than the return of the old painting. It's possible I'm biased.

Locke

DELILAH WATCHED IVAN PETROVICH step toward her on the pier made ghostly by the night time gloom. "Don't take it personally, Miss Samson," he said, broken nose still purple from where she'd punched him a week before. "It's not that we don't like you."

"A lot," his companion added. She'd never learned his name. His file was marked 'Snail' because he was always trailing the rest of the gang. "I'd get your autograph if you weren't handcuffed."

A freezing wind whipped the snow at her feet as Delilah smiled. "Take 'em off, big boy. I bet we can find a pen."

Snail stared, confusion clouding his round face.

Ivan shook his head in frustration. "No. You stay handcuffed, we stay alive. We've been over this."

"This is overkill," Delilah said as icy spray from Lake Michigan bit her ankle. If they pushed her in the water it would be merely waste disposal. With the arctic front that had moved in, all they needed to do to kill her was to leave her outside for another hour.

"You're asking the wrong kinds of questions. Hanging with the wrong kind of people," Ivan said. "I bet your parents warned you about talking to strangers."

"Not as such, no." The shackles around her feet were making life difficult. Ivan had welded them shut before she woke from whatever drug they'd used to give her such a stupendous headache. If she wasn't careful, she was going to lose both her feet tonight. Or her life. She glanced over her shoulder at the water and tried to figure out if the heat from the broken shackles would be tempered enough by the chill of the water to escape with only third degree burns. Physics had never been her favorite subject. "I really think this is a bad plan, boys. If we go through with this, what will we have to do next time we meet? You're escalating the problem. All I want to know is what hit the street. I hate being left out."

Ivan grabbed the lapel of her woolen dress coat, pushing her back so she balanced on her Miu Miu heels. "You should have stayed out of it."

"Don't make me kill you, Ivan. You know what the dry cleaners charge. We go to the same place. Mr. Way is not going to be happy about this."

"But the boss will be. Goodnight, sweetheart." He moved to kiss her and Delilah kicked back, pulling him down into the water with her.

Cold wasn't the right word. Cold was snowflakes, or iced tea, or the look in her mother's eyes when anyone mentioned Colorado. Lake Michigan in mid-December was a crypt. Death circled, numbing her to the bone. Water poured down her throat as she reflexively gasped for air. Be a mutant freak. Try to save the world. Die of drowning.

Heat burst around her as the shackles fell away. Maybe three seconds had passed. The freezing water had numbed her soul right out of her body. She could almost see herself in the dark water, feebly trying to claw to the surface but sinking anyway because her muscles couldn't move.

Mom is never going to forgive me for this.

The murky darkness of the water became an air-filled darkness bursting with pain, cold limbs brought to warmth and burning from the change of temperature. Freezing water filled her mouth, her lungs... Air.

There was air!

There was the sensation of someone holding her close, and then her knees slammed onto something too hard to be the muddy lake bottom.

Delilah choked, coughed, and vomited out polluted water onto a moonlight-smeared wood floor that bobbed up and down.

None of those words made sense. She made a living out of being sensible, politically aware, and biting her tongue. And yet the floor was bobbing at her. "Th-that's n' ri'." Her teeth chattered. So unbearably cold. Pain. Cold. Heat. Darkness. Movement. She looked up at a shadow, searching for the man it belonged to—but there was no man. No light. Only a shadow. She forced her arms to hug herself for the relief it offered. "'Elp?"

"I can get you a blanket," the shadow said.

"'Es." Hot tears burned her face. She was alive.

Anger burst through the pain. Ivan was going to regret this night for the rest of his foreshortened life. She'd make sure of that.

Ivan. Snail. The mayor. In her mind she lined up the rogue's gallery. Dealing drugs out of rehab centers, now that took a twisty kind of mind. The city tried to reduce street crime by sending minor offenders to weekend rehabilitation instead of jail, and what did those hoodlums go home with? A nice duffle bag full of pamphlets, clean underwear, and dime bags of meth.

But something more was happening. The thriving Chicago sub-economy had gone quiet in the past few weeks, like birds before a storm. Or the jungle when an apex predator stalked past. She thought she'd finally caught a break when Ivan and Snail scheduled a meet down on West Wacker. All the evidence was on the camera... The camera!

She struggled to stand and started stripping off her wet clothes. If the camera was ruined... *Argh! Ivan you idiot, why couldn't you off me in the normal way?* His modus operandi was leaving people "drunk" and stripped in one of the parks. The cops logged it as a partygoer who'd wandered off and been killed by Chicago's infamous weather. It happened. It was a shame. No crime though. Why'd he have to change his style now?

Because you're a freak, she reminded herself. The usual drugs didn't affect her strange body chemistry.

"Um..." The man's voice was behind her. "I found a towel if you want... Should I leave?" he asked as she threw her shirt to the side and slid out of her pants.

Pocket. Fingers. Cold fingers never worked the way she wanted. Why couldn't the goons have been operating in Miami? This was it. This was definitely going to be her last winter in Chicago. In March she'd ask for the raise and a transfer to the Subrosa Securities offices somewhere warm. The French Riviera maybe. Or Spain. Or... somewhere. She wiggled out of her boots and dug her fingers into the lining where she'd slid the ultra-thin camera as soon as she'd realized someone was following her. *Hot dog!* With shaking hands she patted it dry. There. Good. Evidence. Now...

Her teeth started chattering again.

A warm, scratchy blanket was laid over her shoulders. Delilah looked down, saw a cord... followed the cord to a little green light.

"Heating blanket," the shadow said. He faded into the corner. "I know you're not a native, but we figure even tourists should know better than to swim in Lake Michigan in the middle of winter. That's why it's not posted on the docks next to the prominent 'Keep Out—Authorized Personnel Only' signs."

Delilah's fist clenched around the camera. "Th-thanks. Silly me." She sucked in cool air. "Where are we?"

"A boat."

Good. Locations were good. "Yours?"

"No."

"Mine?"

"Not that I'm aware of."

All right then. She nodded. "Phone?"

"I don't keep one on me. Makes me feel like I'm wearing a leash. It's good to get away from the day job, don't you think?"

She gave him her best *shut up* glare, perfected on her four siblings over the past two decades, and staggered toward a wall. Walls meant doors. Doors meant halls. Halls meant communications devices of some kind. Boats had phones, or computers, or radios, something like that. Her sum knowledge of boats was they were supposed to float, holes were bad, and boats talked to other boats. Ergo, help and warm clothes were just down the hall. And possibly up a flight of stairs.

"Where are you going?" the shadow asked.

"Help. Got to get help." She huffed on her cupped hands to keep them warm. There was a pop behind her as the heating blanket came unplugged from the hall. How inconvenient.

The shadow bent down and plugged it back in. "Sit down. I'll go find a phone. And some clothes."

A real gentleman would have offered his coat. Not that her mysterious rescuer seemed to have one. If he was who she was beginning to suspect he was, he didn't need one. Ghosts didn't need anything to keep the chill off.

Delilah sat on a vinyl bench and looked at the city skyline through a narrow rectangular window. Willis

Tower was lit up for the holidays, bright, festive, and a beacon of hope north of her. So, 31st Street Harbor. Good. The cab could be here in a matter of minutes. She leaned back.

"Got a problem here," said the shadow as he entered the room. "The clothes are a bit big and these shoes..." He held up a pair of bright pink satin pumps in a lady's size twenty. Both her feet could have fit in one with room left over.

"Everyone needs a hobby." The words came out clearly between her chattering teeth. "Phone?"

"Nothing. I guess whoever comes here likes their privacy."

"Fine. I'll walk. Give me the clothes."

He held out a matching pink-sequined dress that was too big, bright, and cheap to ever be in her wardrobe.

"And here I thought I'd have to join the circus to wear something this tacky." At least the sleeves were long. Too long. Like an over-sized sweater made in the middle of a sequin explosion. "Thanks for the lift. It was nice not seeing you. Enjoy your evening." She pulled the heating blanket's plug deliberately this time, folded the blanket neatly, and made a mental note to send one of the interns down to the docks with a small remuneration and the dress for the owner.

"Mind telling me what you were up to tonight?" The shadow followed her down the creaky hall.

"Chasing bad guys, busting drug deals, getting evidence. You know, do-gooder stuff."

"You think you're a superhero?"

Ha. "Nope. You are though, right? The Spirit of Chicago, our city's favorite son. I saw the news segment you did in the graveyard last year. No record of birth, no name, no physical body, although you've just demonstrated your ability to lift things up, so I have to wonder how much of that was staged."

The shadows where his face should have been changed, shading to mimic the expression of a surprised man. "Says the woman who impersonates Harry Houdini as a Christmas Party trick." He sighed. "What's your name?"

"At home?"

The *Rosencrantz and Guildenstern* reference flew right over his head. "On your Company file."

"Locke." She smiled sweetly over her shoulder. "But I'm not listed as a superhero."

"The villain?" He swore so softly she would have missed it if she weren't expecting it.

"That's me."

"What are you doing chasing drug dealers? Did they cut you out of something?"

Delilah rolled her eyes. "No, I was chasing them because you suck at your job. Your ability to catch actual criminals is matched only by your ability to stop time and speed up the harvest. You've never done anything but haunt people." She leaned against the rail. "Do you know what time it is?"

"Hot date?"

"No." Her date was lukewarm at best, and being stood up for the third time. Hopefully the mayor's right-hand man would get the point. Every time she ran into him, she fought the urge to stab his eyes out of spite. Alan Adale was the snake of Eden walking around in the body of a fallen angel. He had asked her if she was free for dinner tonight in front of people. There'd been no way to wiggle out of it without losing her standing. Besides, the local tabloids already had them pegged as Chicago's next Power Couple, as if that was something to be proud of. She was pretty sure Adale was up to his handsome neck in whatever was going down. "Time?"

"Quarter to eleven. You missed *Doctor Who*, but you should be able to catch a rerun of the *Firefly* reboot."

"Unlikely. I need to catch a plane. My intern is flying in," she elaborated when he tilted his head.

"Super villains have interns?"

"Well, superheroes have the whole sidekick thing pretty well wrapped up. I guess you could call him a minion, but since he's being paid instead of exploited, I went with intern." And if she missed his flight and left her sister's favorite student of all time stranded at O'Hare airport... Angela had doted on the boy even before he'd shot her in the arm. When he'd come to Angela's wedding over the summer, he'd mentioned he was having weird premonitions. Like called to like. Delilah'd asked some questions and, sure enough, Big Sis's favorite kid was a genetic freak too. His powers were minor, premonitions of when people were going to die and the ability to heal a little faster than normal humans. It wasn't enough to win him a spot in The Company as a superhero, but it would be enough to earn him a visit from their silencing squad if they ever found out about him.

Delilah and Angela's family had closed ranks around the boy, herding him in like they had Angela's husband and brother-in-law. Travys was safe. And once he'd enrolled in the University of Chicago, she'd pulled a few strings to get him a place as her intern for a few months. It was the only way to train him to survive.

The shadow sauntered closer. "Where do you need to go? I can drop you off at home."

"I don't take boys home on the first date, or ghosts home ever. My ride will be here shortly."

An icy breeze fluttered her hair. Behind the shadow a man in a tight blue suit landed, face covered by a sculpted mask that horribly disfigured the handsome man beneath. Not the ride she'd expected. "My ears are burning. Were you talking about me?" the man asked with a smile.

She could picture Ty raising an eyebrow behind his mask.

"Cute dress," her brother-in-law said. "Angela will be jealous."

"Long story. How'd you know I needed a lift?"

"Frederick called to tell us you were out of communication. I came out and waited. Who's the new boyfriend?"

"The Spirit of Chicago, and not my boyfriend." She walked over to her brother-in-law, waving careless fingers over her shoulder. "Toodles."

The shadow gave her a lazy salute. "Some other time, perhaps."

"Perhaps."

Ty moved fast, dropping her at the apartment and flying her to the airport once she'd changed. He hovered in the shadows. "You sure you're fine?"

"I'm perfect. No lingering affects except an abiding desire to get home and snuggle under my quilt with the heater turned up to eighty. Freddie is bringing the cab around. I'll drop Travys at his dorm room and go straight home. Which is where you should go," she added firmly. "Your home. Drop the camera off with Daddy on your way, please."

He laughed. "You need to go get your own errand boy."

"I have twelve minions and an intern who eats like a horse."

"Why don't you co-opt that shadow dude? He's here, why can't he work for us?"

Delilah smiled wryly. "Us being the good guys who fight the other good guys for a chance to fight the bad guys? There is no 'us', Ty. Maybe you and Angela have California tied up, but the Midwest isn't going to suddenly see the light and flee the strangling embrace of The Company. I'm not sure the Spirit of Chicago could. He's supposed to be the ghost of someone who died in the Chicago fire."

"He looked solid to me."

"Yeah." To her too. "I'll worry about it later. Kisses to Angela, tell Aaron I say hi."

"No more adventures before Christmas," Ty said. "Angela's been sleeping poorly enough as it is."

"Oh?" Delilah glanced up, although Ty's masked face gave no hints.

He shrugged. "Nightmares about what happened with Jacob. She wakes up screaming about fires. Not frequent, but between that and the stomach bug going around it's been a rough week."

She nodded. "No more adventures. Promise. I will not do anything thrilling, heroic, or risky for the next two weeks. Girl Scout's honor." A plane rumbled overhead, coming in to land. "That should be Travys. Have a good night." She smiled and walked into the lobby before Ty could remember she'd never been a Girl Scout.

The warm, stale air of the terminal was almost comforting. Still, she shivered. Nightmares were the bane of her existence. First her mother's memories of the time she was kidnapped and mind-raped in Colorado, and now her sister's memories of the man she couldn't save. She'd un-locked those, stolen them in unguarded moments, and they'd become part of her even though they weren't her experiences. A midnight swim in Lake Michigan just couldn't compete. So she tucked the fear out of the way, and moved forward. A super villain's work was never done.

CHAPTER TWO

Dear Dad,

I need a new watch for Christmas. Waterproof. Possibly with a miniaturized Agree-With-Me ray attached. You know, for the days when I run into trouble. I also need new boots. Mine got wet.

Your daughter who is glad she took swimming lessons,

Delilah

THE SPIRIT OF CHICAGO leaned his head against a cold brick wall and stared out over the dark harbor. That had gone as badly as he could have imagined anything going. Delilah Samson. What a gal.

In the city's complex world of politics, crime, and money, he'd had her pegged as a lady on the lowest rung. He knew her, of course; Subrosa Securities was a big name in private safety and Delilah Samson the beautiful treat they trotted out like a show pony for all their affluent clients. She'd even run point a few times, hovering near various Subrosa clients at charity balls and holiday mixers with a slightly detached expression, while the men tripped over themselves to get her attention. Gorgeous. That's all anyone ever remembered. Delilah Samson hadn't been born, she'd been carved from alabaster. Her eyes were luminous topaz, deep, dark, and radiant. Her dark chocolate hair fell in waves to her hips, begging men and women alike to imagine her lying in their beds with a sated smile.

Or maybe that was just him.

He'd known she was involved with that idiot Ivan as well, if involved meant they sometimes traded cool glances at the dry cleaners. He was willing to strangle Ivan for that alone, stealing her time and favor—and then tonight. The one night he'd felt reasonably certain Miss Samson would be safe, she wasn't. His plans for the evening had gone to hell in a burning hand basket when the little radar he'd illegally pinned on Ivan's car met with the one on Boris Lugchevka's car. Boris was a thug with a list of petty convictions stretching back to his childhood in the late nineties. Ivan was the brains, maybe even a major player in the criminal underworld, it was hard to say. He had no arrest record. No proof he'd ever done anything wrong. But he was always on the fringe of criminal activity, and if Ivan didn't commit crimes, he certainly wouldn't hesitate to egg Boris on.

The Spirit had arrived at the dock in time to see Delilah fall into the water. Searching the dark lake with nothing but hope and the faint impressions left by shadows was not the way to conduct a rescue operation in the dead of winter. He'd thought he'd lost her.

That was why he'd made so many mistakes. Bringing her to the nearest yacht seemed safe enough. She'd looked so helpless, dark eyes huge and filled with fear, her long hair tangled by the lake water, so he'd stayed to offer help. A normal woman would have been too shaken to do anything but thank him. Not Delilah. No, she noticed he picked up a towel. She'd identified him. She was evaluating him.

A beautiful, brainy woman.

She was going to be the death of him.

He sighed and ran his hands through his short hair as his physical body reformed around him. For thirteen years he'd kept his secret safe. Everyone, from The Company superheroes to the local media, accepted the fact that The Spirit of Chicago was a ghost.

After all, why not? When the evening news was filled with accounts of a man who could turn into an eight- foot giant with bark for skin, a ghost seemed downright normal.

When he'd first approached The Company, a seemingly typical reckless and angry teenager, he'd been wary. He'd been scared of what they might do with him if they knew his name. So he'd lied.

The United States government's clandestine superhero control unit didn't know his real name or what he looked like. They were content believing he was a ghost, an incorporeal man without the ability to touch, pick up, or manipulate anything. He watched people. Sometimes he frightened people. But really he was an informer, a Company spy.

And because he'd picked up a towel, Delilah Samson knew more about him than anyone in thirteen years.

The real question was: What else did she know? Could she guess from his voice who he was? Would she guess? And if she guessed, what then? Blackmail? Vows of secrecy? A kiss to thank him next time they met wearing their business faces?

His heart raced, half agony, half hope. Maybe he could find a way to tell her without losing the life he'd so carefully cultivated since escaping the hell of his childhood. Integrate her. Convince her to ally with him and keep Chicago safe.

Wishful thinking, he admitted as he walked into his apartment and locked the door. They'd barely exchanged half a dozen civil words with each other and he was ready to name the date, the kids, and the hypothetical dog.

Tossing his watch on the kitchen counter, The Spirit of Chicago stalked back to what he liked to call The Lair: his apartment's spare bedroom retrofitted with bulletproof glass, heavy curtains to keep out prying eyes, and an entire wall devoted to visualizing the dynamics of Chicago's power players.

Mayor Marco Arámbula occupied one pyramid of power. Chief of Police Brian Wyte owned his own pyramid too; he'd gained ground in the last year and the next election was looking like it might be a run-off between Arámbula and Wyte. The crime syndicates were smaller blobs formed under a big question mark. Ten years ago the individual gangs still had power—some, at any rate. The police force whittled that away and into the power vacuum a new player crept. The gangs and the Outfit had become mere feeder streams to the one big boss.

There was no name to go with the question mark. Not yet. But he'd have it soon enough. He needed the name before the criminal element in Chicago became too organized and efficient to break without going to war.

The Spirit of Chicago traced a finger down the pyramid of power under Wyte. Subrosa Securities worked in happy harmony with the police force, so he'd put Delilah Samson right down at the bottom with the other peons. Only—his finger paused—she wasn't there. Huh.

He checked his desk drawer and after a quick search found a magnet, purple for a reason he couldn't fathom, with a black and white image of her face glued on it. Hesitating only for a moment, he placed Delilah on the third tier under Chief Wyte.

She wouldn't report directly to him, but her boss had to know.

Subrosa had a good deal if she really had super-powers. They could offer her protection from The Company and other less pleasant groups that might want to take advantage of someone with super mutations, and she had free license to use her skills. He grabbed a scanner and read the barcode under her picture.

He turned his computer on to read the cross-referenced files. *Let's see...* Delilah Samson, age twenty-six, height five ten, born in 2007, hired by Subrosa Securities in the spring of 2029 at age twenty-four. He scrolled down and stared at a blank page.

Nothing.

Delilah Samson sprang into being five years ago? He doubted that. Logic said she had a family somewhere, a history, school records. People left tracks.

He pulled up the Subrosa Securities website first, scrolling through their list of employees all for hire as discreet service or to set up your next security system. How embarrassing. As if security guards were some kind of accessory you picked to match your shoes in the morning.

Three pages in, he hit the end of the Bodyguards For Hire and still hadn't found Miss Samson. He checked the personnel listings for secretaries, hostesses, and other office minions. Not a trace of his delinquent Delilah.

Grumbling in frustration, he pulled up the president's information. Wilford Andrews, a bespectacled and impossibly fit man with gray hair and dark skin stared sternly back. Andrews was the regional president and head of Midwestern operations (USA) for Subrosa. And there, under the title 'Vice President', was Delilah Samson, resplendent in a blood-red jacket and skirt. She should have looked like a bellhop, but instead her flat stare seemed to oscillate between a come-hither invitation and the cold warning that she would not hesitate to put a bullet in your head.

He loosened his collar and opened up Andrew's file. Yale graduate, law school, served in the army JAG for twenty years before retiring to the civil sector and joining Subrosa fifteen years ago. Delilah? Nothing. No background, no schools listed, no experience.

No super villain alive had such a weak cover story. Most the ones he'd met had not just one backstory, but several alter egos with the paperwork to prove who they were. And super villains didn't play the role of neighborhood vigilante. That was strictly a Good Guy thing.

So, what? She was FBI maybe? CIA? Some other black-ops government group who needed a plant and thought no one would check her cover story? Homeland Security might try to pull something like that. Or the DoD. Although they could have at least made some effort to make sure her history passed a cursory inspection.

Unless she wasn't meant to pass inspection. Maybe she was bait.

His head started to hurt. Would it kill people to just tell him the truth? A little up front honesty was all he wanted. "Hi, my name's Delilah and I was trained by assassin monks in Antarctica to fight the hordes of rabid polar bears descending from Canada."

Or not. He shut off the computer as an email popped up on his work account. That could wait until morning. Right now he needed to wash the reminder of Lake Michigan—and Delilah Samson—off his skin.

CHAPTER THREE

Dear Daddy,

Yes, I have every intention of visiting the 'Splendor of Gems' display at the museum when it comes to town. There's an event there tonight, coincidentally. Or not: I suspect it's because of this fact that you emailed me while you should have been lecturing the freshman of the University of Texas about the dangers of uncontrolled experiments.

I'll ignore the news headlines about the rocket your students made last week if you ignore my social life, or lack thereof. Deal?

Busiest,
Delilah

"YOU LOOK BETTER," TRAVYS said as he walked into Delilah's office carrying a shoebox and kicked the door shut behind him. "And you don't smell like sewage."

"I told you, I fell in the lake."

Her intern looked skeptical and slightly thuggish in his Chicago Bull's leather jacket.

"We need to get you a trench coat."

Travys pursed his lips and shook his head rapidly. "Chicago Gangster is not a good fashion on boys from the hood."

"Neither is a leather sports jacket that looks like you stole it during a fan frenzy."

"I like it." He stroked the sleeve and pouted. "The red brings out my eyes. Gem tones always do."

She paused, then raised an eyebrow at his mocking tone. "When did I say that?"

"When you had to go to the fall harvest ball thing in a red dress like some overpriced assassin."

Delilah leaned back. "Oh, the Dior. I looked amazing."

"Yes," Travys agreed with a very masculine smile, at odds with his still-boyish face.

She wagged a finger at him. "None of that. Baby brothers are supposed to play with LEGOs and cars, not ogle girls."

"I'm not formally adopted," Travys protested.

"Don't argue semantics with an expert, kid. As far as the Powers That Be are concerned, you're my baby brother and I shall treat you as such. No girl will ever be good enough. Your room will never be clean enough. And I will question your personal style on a thrice-weekly basis."

"Thrice?" His eyebrows rose. "Thrice? Really? Thrice?"

Delilah shrugged. "It's the appropriate word."

"Yeah. I bet. You know, my English professor at the college is single. Want me to find out if he's available for New Year's Eve?" Travys gave her a grin that bordered on a leer. "Maybe you could 'thrice' each other a bit."

She picked up the hot chocolate on her desk. "You see this? My aim is amazing." She gave him a warning look and sipped the cocoa. "So, what's in the box?"

"Uh-uh," Travys said with a shake of his head. "Tell me why you weren't out with Alan 'Mister Amazing' Adale last night. The date was on your calendar."

"I skipped it to play footsie with some hoodlums. What's in the box?"

"What's wrong with Adale?" Travys persisted. "Is he a skanky-manwhore? Does he have a disease?"

In town for less than twenty-four hours and already he was scrutinizing her social life. "Did my sister write this script for you? Because for a second there, I could have sworn you were Angela."

Travys rolled his eyes.

She exhaled, setting her mug down. "He's too good to be true. I dated a boy like him in high school. Halfway through our second date I slipped a little. I wanted him to tell me why he liked me and since I was sixteen and could make him be honest... he was."

"How bad was it?"

Delilah tightened her grip on the mug. "He asked me out because I was almost as hot as my sister, and he heard I was easy." She shrugged as if it didn't matter anymore. "I don't need a repeat experience."

Travys eyed her thoughtfully. "What if Adale actually likes you?"

Delilah laughed. "What if Neptune is made of green cheese?" She shook her head. "Men are not attracted to me for my personality. They think short skirts mean I'm open to the idea of a one-night stand. Forgive me for being a little gun-shy. Now, what's in the box?"

"Some of my mom's stuff. A couple of bills from after she left, a note from my grandma, an invite to the school's parent night." He pushed the shoebox across her desk until it bumped into a pile of papers.

"How'd your dad take your visit home?"

"He's not my dad," Travys said as he sat down. "He's a loser. A dick that stood up for me once in his entire life." He glared out her window for a minute, then shrugged. "He's back in jail. He got caught with some dime bags. Stupid. I mean... dime bags? He makes trash look classy."

Delilah didn't contradict him. Chris Freeman was the kind of man parents prayed their child would never meet: charismatic, abusive, and self-centered as a spinning top. His motivation lasted right up until he had cash to burn, and then he was gone. Travy's mom had kept them from living in the street by working double shifts at a hair salon and sometimes picking up temp work at the call center for New York's cab companies. She'd been missing since spring of 2032, when Chris had gotten out of jail and Travys had tried to commit suicide.

Angela, Delilah's older sister, had saved Travys' life and taken a bullet to her arm for the trouble. But Travys was a bright kid; he'd finished school and graduated with a GPA that earned him a full ride scholarship to the University of Chicago.

"What are you doing with the house?"

He twitched a shoulder. "Nothing. I'm not sure who even owns it, so I just cleared out my stuff and Mom's. Chris can make the payments if he wants to keep it." He scuffed his foot on the ground. "She's not coming back."

"Who? Your mom? No, I think at this point it's safe to say she isn't planning to return to New York." Delilah lifted the lid of the box and placed the contents in front of her.

"She's dead," Travys said with absolute certainty in his voice.

Delilah looked up at him questioningly. "What makes you say that?"

"Same thing that told me Wiley Johnson wasn't going to make it through high school alive. Every time I saw him, I couldn't see it. I couldn't picture him in the cap and gown, you know? He was the nicest guy, super smart, funny, everybody liked him. And then some drunk hit him walking home from school. Three in the afternoon. Bright light. Crosswalk. The driver ran over him like he was a speed bump.

"It's the same thing now. I can't picture my mom coming back to me. I'm never going to see her again. Never." His voice caught, the edge of a sob peeking out.

"I'm sorry."

His eyes narrowed. "Did you know?"

"I guessed." She sighed. "Travys, your mom is a won-derful person. I have utmost respect for her, but she's also the perfect victim: alone, scared, vul-nerable... Female," she added. "She was on the run, and no one knew where she was. Isolation makes a person an easy target. The fewer people who know where they are, the fewer people will notice them missing."

He frowned, lips trembling as he bit back more tears. After a minute he said, "Do you think—do you think she wanted to come back? She didn't, like, make herself stay gone?"

Delilah tried to catch his eye, but Travys was staring resolutely at the wall behind her. "You filled out your mother's personality profile yourself, and your grandma verified it. She didn't have the mentality to be a suicide. If she was going to do something like that, she would have done it years earlier. No." Delilah shook her head. "I think she ran home to Atlanta to get help, planned on coming back for you, and something unexpected happened. Right now, all we have is conjecture. Who knows? Chris going to jail could be the best thing to happen. If she's out there, she might finally feel safe enough to try to contact you again."

"She's dead," Travys said flatly. "I know it."

"In that case, we'll find the person who killed her and make them pay." Delilah shifted into his field of vision and waited until he made eye contact. "You're family, Travys. We will make them pay."

There was a knock at the door and her boss walked in. Wil looked between them. "Am I interrupting something?"

"Travys misfiled a client folder," Delilah said with a dismissive wave. "Typical new-intern troubles. I'm telling you, we should have a boot camp for them. Make Margo in the front office run them through alphabetizing and stapling practice before we unleash them to touch my files. It would save me so much trouble."

Wil shrugged. "Margo doesn't like the interns any more than you do." He tossed a padded tablet onto her desk. "Addison Mayfield called, she's back in town and wants priority security at the soiree she's attending tonight. Go check the venue. I'll arrange the team."

"Am I running point again?" Delilah asked as she opened Addison's folder. The spoiled socialite didn't need security, she needed a babysitter. Possibly a muzzle. Addison attracted trouble like flowers attracted bees.

"You'll be inside with Emerret, Dylan, and Emelia doing perimeter. Chad will have a three-man crew in the comms van. If the intern's free," Wil said, pointing to Travys, "you can take him along. He can shadow Dylan for most of the evening, get an idea of how these things go."

Delilah turned to Travys. "Can you do that, or do you need to study?"

"I'm good. The only final I'm taking is in English, and that's next Thursday." He grinned. "Where we going?"

"A place where you'll need a suit and proper grammar." Delilah smiled up at her boss. "I'll have the walk through done before lunch and be waiting for Addison to arrive at eight."

"I knew you'd be happy about this," Wil said.

Delilah let that one slide. Private security was the bread-and-butter of Subrosa Security. Addison might have been spoiled, but for a security team this large she was shelling out over a quarter of a million dollars for six hours of work. The salary was good, and the commission for working one of these jobs made it possible to buy all the finer things in life. "Come on, let's head down to the museum."

"The where?" Travys asked, following her out the door that swung shut and locked without being touched.

She picked her coat off the office coat-tree. "The Field Museum. They're opening a display of the world's largest gems tonight with a charity fundraiser. Tickets start in the five-hundred-dollar range. Dinner and drinks are another thousand. With the mid-term elections coming up, there will be a lot of schmoozing."

"I like schmoozing," Travys said agreeably.

Delilah cut him a look. "They won't be schmoozing us. We'll be the polite backdrop and stay out of the way." She checked her watch. "Can you meet me there in thirty minutes? I have a little errand to run now that the dry cleaner is open."

"Sure thing, boss."

Rolling her eyes, Delilah left Travys to find transportation for himself and took a cab over to Way Quick Cleaning, proprietor Mister Lee Way. The cab driver hunched over in his seat, a large flat cap covering his bulbous head. "I won't be a moment," she told him as she stepped out, not bothering to pay.

Having a super villain as a daddy came with certain perks. Freddie, the cab driver, was one of them. Her favorite minion, he was a five-foot-tall frog crossed with who-knew-what-else, made in her father's lab. Completely dependable, able to drive, and good for tossing people around when she needed some muscle, the whole not-paying-cab-fares was a welcome bonus.

Mr. Way looked up from his e-print subscription tablet as she walked in. "Good morning, Miss Samson. Do you have something to drop off?"

"I do." She held up a long, thin envelope. "Remember Ivan, the tall Russian with the dark hair?"

"The one with the bunged up nose?" Mr. Way frowned. "I'm not getting caught in a lover's quarrel."

"It's nothing like that. Just business."

"I don't like that any better," he said, refusing to reach for the envelope.

"All I'm asking you to do is stick this in his pocket."

"How do you know I even have one his suits in?"

"Because Ivan's a very particular man, and this morning he would have brought in a slightly damp suit that looked he tried to wash it in Lake Michigan."

Mr. Way's eyebrows shot up in surprise. "How'd you hear about that?"

"It's better if I don't go into detail." She pushed the envelope across the counter. "Tuck this into his pocket, please? And don't bother mentioning it to Ivan. It's nothing important." Before Mr. Way could object, Delilah laid two hundred-dollar bills on the counter with a wink. "Have a good day, Mr. Way."

CHAPTER FOUR

Dear Daddy,

No, I won't bring you home any gems as a party favor. Not even the emerald.

Tsk tsk,
Delilah

DELILAH LEFT ADDISON MAYFIELD surrounded by a crowd of gawkers and circulated around the room. As a rule the Field Museum had excellent security, decent catering, and plenty of exquisite objects that made her itch for a little larceny. If she had somewhere to stash a T. Rex, Sue's skeleton would already be in her apartment. As it was, she'd already bought the limited edition miniature Sue the museum was selling to fund whatever it was they'd been funding. Her eyes had glazed over at that point of the welcome speech.

These nights were all the same. Come in, spend cash, meet other rich people, talk shop, and drink moderately cheap wine. Eleven o'clock couldn't come fast enough.

It was strange that the research gene had skipped her so thoroughly. Daddy and Gideon would have been absolutely enraptured listening to someone yammer endlessly about a new expansion to the labs. She'd been more distracted by the sparkling exhibits in the Hall of Gems. In one corner the Moussaieff Red glittered near the Agra diamonds. The Heart of Eternity sat beside the Millennium Sapphire, beautiful blue-toned rainbows dancing around them. The star of the show sat in the center of the room on a lit plinth: the faceted, twenty-five pound emerald called Teodora.

Large as a watermelon, the Teodora certainly had an eye-catching quality. Delilah circled it lazily, keeping half an eye on Addison while admiring the craftsmanship that had gone into refining the giant stone. Flawless, time-consuming work. A galaxy of lighter colors rifted through the dark green inside of the gem. Mesmerizing.

Other people started filing in, champagne glasses in hand. Without turning from the emerald, Delilah looked for the telltale bulge or crease in a jacket that would give away a concealed weapon.

"The first protestors have arrived," Chad whispered over her concealed earpiece. "None of them are on the watch list for the client."

Delilah nodded, certain that Chad would see her on the cameras. The price of discretion was leaving her voice pickup with Travys for the evening. He was under strict instructions to come find her at the first whiff of trouble.

Protestors weren't trouble, though; they were simply the accouterments of Chicago politics. Half of them were probably paid to make a mini-riot for the evening news and would leave within the hour. See and be seen. Stir up some interest, stir up some cash. The politicians would use the attention to woo new backers for whatever pet project they wanted funded next.

If anyone else had been paying attention they would have guessed the political structure of the city in less than ten minutes. Although Mayor Arámbula was conspicuous in his absence, his snake-eyed second-in-command, Alan Adale, was present and making the rounds. The moment she made eye contact he moved in like a heat-seeking missile.

She walked around the plinth, avoiding eye contact. The first time they'd met, Delilah had carefully filed him away as Too Dangerous To Handle. Lucifer had probably cried hot tears of envy when Adale was born. He had a sculpted masculine perfection and confident swagger that made everyone want to fall to their knees in worship, and one close encounter had been enough to send her scrambling for safety. She'd canceled every date, evaded him at every turn. But, like the devilish predator he was, he kept circling.

Pretty soon she'd need to whip out the big guns and flat out break his heart. Tease him on a little, then drop him like a rock. Dent his ego so he never bounced back her way again. After all, breaking hearts was far more fun than finding out she was just another anonymous booty call.

Adale stopped next to the display case, not completely immune to her 'Don't talk to me' glare. He feigned interest in the cushion-cut American Golden Topaz, glancing at the gem then up at her. Caught staring, Delilah turned away and focused on the Teodora. Lines of lighter green seemed to be moving in the smaragdine depths, rolling like waves before coalescing into spheres like eyes. Two large, bulbous eyes, blinking out at her from inside the Teodora.

Delilah almost gasped. The size of the gem was right, but the color was unusual, as was the texture. Minion eggs were traditionally more gelatinous. Comfy, too. She'd used an egg mass as a reading chair one summer in high school.

The black and bronze display tag said the Teodora had been discovered in Brazil, cut in India, and had a cloud of rumors surrounding its authenticity. In the end, it had been donated to the Smithsonian by the beleaguered owner.

Brazil... Brazil... Daddy had taken them down there one summer when she was six or so. He'd done a week of guest lecturing at one of the universities, and they'd spent another month exploring the humid country while avoiding a cold snap in Texas. All she remembered was a blur of spontaneous decisions that spoke volumes about her mother's unwillingness to sit through a Texas ice storm.

Considering the haphazard nature of life in the years after her mother's kidnapping and return, it wasn't hard to imagine Daddy losing an experiment. Or even leaving it behind on purpose. He probably thought it would be a fun joke.

"Beautiful," said a low, very masculine voice behind her.

Delilah spun on her heel, professional smile firmly in place. "It's a stunning gem."

The deputy mayor looked down at her with cool green eyes. "I wasn't talking about the stone."

A fission of fear climbed up her spine. It was uncomfortable being the center of his focus. Most people were lazy; they chatted and grew distracted and never seemed to be really watching her. Adale's emotionless gaze focused on her like a searchlight, stripping away the layers of deceit she used for protection. It was terrifying. He definitely had a future with the mob if the whole political career thing didn't work out.

"You're too kind." Delilah took him by the arm and steered him away from the Teodora. "Have you been enjoying your evening?"

"It's been uneventful so far. I missed having dinner with you last night."

"An emergency at work. I did leave you a message."

His hand covered hers. "Nothing terribly taxing I trust."

Her pulse fluttered as his eyes filled with concern. "It left me with a bit of a headache, but I survived." She wanted to unleash her skills on him there and then, drown him in the need to tell the truth and end the charade. But the political fallout of an honest evening would turn Chi-cago into a battleground. So she ground her teeth and kept the battle inside, reminding herself that she couldn't trust him no matter how genuine he seemed.

"I didn't bother rescheduling the reservations," Adale said, removing his hand from hers. "Your work seems to keep you busy at every hour I can invent. Although, I confess, seeing you here improves my day considerably. This would be a dreary party without you."

His smile cut through her like a laser. She shot him her own, full of knives. "Oh, I doubt that's true. You were dancing attendance on Perri Lang earlier this evening." Perri Lang, modern-day Lucrezia Borgia, whose father's chemical plant and research labs only avoided closure because he greased palms throughout the city. Where money didn't work rumor held his daughter's attentions did.

Adale grinned self-depreciatingly. "Yes, I spoke with her. It was even less educational than usual, but I'm glad you noticed."

"I didn't notice."

He raised an eyebrow as they stopped in front of a display of rings. "You said you saw me with Miss Lang."

"I'm here with Addison Mayfield. Miss Lang and Miss Mayfield are..." Delilah search for the right words.

"Rivals?" Adale suggested.

Delilah exhaled. "More like two cats in heat fighting over a tom. Keeping them in the same county is a recipe for trouble. If I can keep them from causing a scene tonight, Addison's father will pay me a bonus." She fought the impulse to roll her eyes.

"How mercenary of you. Tell me, will the bonus be enough to allow you to take a week's vacation? Maybe linger over a meal or two?"

"No." She glanced back at the Teodora and the eyes watching her. Minion biology wasn't her specialty, but if she recalled the development correctly, eyes appeared in the week before hatching.

Adale sighed. "You seem distracted. Am I boring you?"

"Hmm? Oh. No." Delilah stopped scanning the room for security cameras. There were still three hours left of the party. Give the crew a few hours to clean up, and she could be back here by three in the morning. Walk in, break the glass, grab the emerald, run out... No, she probably needed to cut the power to the cameras first. Infuriating.

"It's all right. I understand if you're not interested. Perhaps you like dark-haired men? I think the head of Alrosa is here, the Russian diamond company. He might be your type. Let's see. Ah, yes, over there in the corner."

Delilah scanned the room and spotted the mustached Russian with Ivan Petrovich at his elbow. If looks could kill, Ivan's would have put her in an early grave.

Adale leaned a little closer. "Why is that gentleman glaring at us? Jealousy, perhaps?"

Ivan's eyes narrowed as he ran a hand down the line of his suit jacket. The very same suit he'd worn the night before. He must have gotten her note.

She winked at Ivan. Time to move the party downstairs where there were more exits. It didn't matter if the deputy mayor looked like a cold-blooded hit man, he wasn't. There would be serious repercussions if she let her two lives cross streams.

Delilah turned to beam at Adale. "Who wouldn't be jealous of me? I have the most handsome man in the room at my side. Let me buy you a drink, to make up for shame-fully neglecting you last night."

Adale's smirk threatened to turn into a smile. "I'm being used, but I don't know what for."

"Enjoy the attention while it lasts," Delilah said, steering him out of the room. Dylan and Travys passed her, casually chatting as they followed Addison.

"Problems?" Chad whispered in her ear.

Delilah nodded, which drew Adale's gaze.

"Something wrong?" he echoed Chad's question with bland amusement.

"Not at all." They walked down the grand staircase like Prince Charming and his sinister Cinderella. Everyone watched. For the first time in her life, Delilah felt like actual arm-candy. Alan Adale had enough force of presence that people looked at him whether they intended to or not, and she was his decoration of the evening.

Miss Lang's ears were probably steaming with rage.

As they approached the open bar surrounded by gossiping socialites, the caterer's door burst open and Detective Morrow stalked in, a man on a mission.

"Deputy Mayor," Morrow said as he made a bee-line for them. "I need to have a word with you."

"Detective." Adale gently untangled his arm from Delilah's. "What an unexpected pleasure."

"Can we step outside for a minute?"

Delilah grabbed two glasses of alcohol and followed. No one had specifically forbidden her from coming along. That made it practically an invitation. The door swung shut behind her and she stopped short as she heard Morrow's voice.

"The mayor is dead."

"Are you sure?" Adale sounded as shocked as she felt.

In the dark, Detective Morrow shook his head. "Alive people have more face left."

CHAPTER FIVE

Dear Daddy,

I need the book on minion hatching and rearing that Hert wrote. I'd also like to see your field and research notes from every trip to Brazil. There's a slight possibility you left an invasive species near an emerald mine. Does that ring any bells?

Don't ask,
D

DELILAH FLOATED THROUGH THE crowded gem room toward Addison with a polite smile frozen in place. Dead mayors, protestors, and hitmen all at the same party was more than her contract covered.

Ivan stepped in front of her. "Miss Samson."

"Hello. Goodbye." She stepped around him.

He followed her. "You need to leave."

"Working on it."

"Town."

Delilah stared up at him. "Excuse me? Was that a threat?"

The couple nearest them turned around. With a brittle smile, she grabbed Ivan's arm hard enough to leave a bruise and pulled him into the corner. "You don't threaten me. Ever. I'm a little too busy to pay you back for last night, but I promise, it's coming."

She turned to go, and he caught her arm. "Delilah." It was a whisper meant for her ears alone. "Trouble is coming to town. A hunter who likes big game. Subrosa doesn't have the resources for this."

With a soft smile that could have melted the coldest hearts, she whispered back, "Drop dead, Ivan. It'll save me the trouble of getting another pair of boots dirty." She batted her eyelashes.

With a few quick strides that stretched the clingy skirt of her gown to its limits, she caught up with her quarry. "Addison, darling, come with me a moment. There's someone you simply must meet." She brushed away the various sycophants and snatched Addison's glass from her hand. The fumes rising up explained Addison's wobbly walk. "Did you bring a flask of vodka again?"

Addison giggled as Dylan and Travys fell in line.

Delilah shoved the glass at her intern. "Drop that with one of the wait staff and meet us at the back door."

"What's going on?" Dylan demanded.

"The blond man in there? That's Ivan Petrovich, a known mob operative. The client's father is rumored to owe them money, and she'd make lovely ransom bait." Grabbing Addison by the shoulders, Delilah steered her to the back door. "We're moving out now. Alert her overnight team. Tell them to meet us at the house."

Addison smiled drunkenly at her. "Kiss me?"

"You're still not my type," Delilah said.

Travys ran up to them carrying everyone's coats. "I grabbed them from the jacket claim," he explained.

Delilah held Addison's coat by the shoulders. Addison stuck her arm in the sleeve on the third try and Delilah zipped her up. As she turned Addison around, Delilah slipped a hand into the coat pocket and palmed the phone she found inside.

Their party made it to the waiting vehicle without trouble, but as soon as Addison sat down she reached for her phone. As everyone else buckled up, Delilah watched the drunk girl check each pocket three times over.

"Problems?" she asked when it was clear Addison had run out of places to search.

"My phone." Addison pouted.

Dylan sighed and rolled his eyes. "It probably dropped out at the coat claim." He reached to unbuckle himself from the front passenger seat.

"I'll get it," Delilah said, holding up a hand. "Go on ahead. I'll be a few minutes behind you."

"I don't like that," Chad said in her ear.

Dylan nodded at Chad's comment. "We shouldn't split up. Addison can wait until morning for her phone, right?"

Addison gasped as if she'd been slapped. "No phone? All night? Are you crazy?"

"It won't take me more than five minutes to find the phone. I'll be right behind you." Delilah waved away Dylan's next argument. "My call. It's okay." She took her earpiece out and tossed it to Travys. "I'll see you in thirty minutes, give or take a stoplight." With a flash of a smile she stepped back into the bitter winter cold.

The car wheels were turning before the door locked. Delilah watched them drive off. In her pocket, she thumbed Addison's phone off. The last thing she needed was the GPS tracking her every movement. The cab which had followed Addison's car pulled up, cabbie hidden by an upturned collar and an oversized flat cap.

"Where to?" Freddie asked as she climbed inside. He turned down the police radio built into the dashboard.

"To wherever the mayor was shot."

* * *

Snow crunched under Delilah's boot as she stepped out of the cab on East Jackson Drive. "Park down by the university," she told Freddie as a voice on the police radio confirmed an ambulance was en route to collect the final remains of Mayor Arámbula.

Buckingham Fountain was beautiful, even late on a winter night. Past the skeletal trees, golden lights illuminated the sparkling water—though the strobe of blue and red from the waiting squad cars rather ruined the romantic affect.

The cab pulled away. Delilah walked through the fresh-fallen snow, drifting across the icy sidewalk with the calm demeanor of someone exactly where they belonged.

At the edge of the square, one of the officers noticed her. "Ma'am, can I help you?" he said stiffly, shining a flashlight at her face.

"No."

He squinted, trying to make out her face under the black top hat she wore. "Did you hear anything? See anything?"

"I didn't." She watched as the ambulance pulled up and paramedics hurried to the body. They lifted the dead mayor onto a stretcher and a scrap of paper fell out of his pocket. The wind caught it, lifting the paper up out of the snow and blowing it toward her.

"Hey!" one of the officers shouted. "Somebody grab that! Gelphi! Catch that!"

Delilah snatched the paper out of the air with a gloved hand. "Here," she held it out to the policeman she assumed was Officer Gelphi. Three barely legible words scrawled across the paper: Kalydon - 77 Wacker.

"Thank you." Gelphi took the paper back with obvious hesitation. "Ma'am, I'm going to ask you to move along. This is a crime scene."

"Of course." News vans were already parking on Lake-shore Drive and she didn't need to be on camera. "Have a good evening." Pivoting on her heel, Delilah strolled back along the snowy streets until her nose was numb. Seventy-seven Wacker was an office building that had been on the market for several months. It wasn't somewhere the mayor would have gone for a party, but a black market business deal? That sounded plausible.

A warm breeze alerted her to company. "Fancy meeting you here," The Spirit of Chicago said.

Delilah stopped, watching him from the corner of her eye. "How did you hear about this?"

"I have friends at the police department. You?"

She shrugged. "I know all the good gossips." She turned to face him, or as much as there was of him. The festively lit streets twinkled through his gossamer body. "Where were you tonight, super-hero?"

"Where were you, do-gooder super villain?"

With a grimace, she shrugged again. "Busy. I have an airtight alibi. Over a hundred people saw me flirting with a handsome man tonight. We didn't get as far as drinks. Disappointing, overall. Your turn."

"I was trying to attract the attention of devastatingly beautiful woman."

Delilah almost laughed. "Oh? How'd that work out for you?"

"She looked right through me."

They turned side by side to watch the paramedics cover the late mayor's body. A chill that had nothing to do with the temperature and everything to do with the muted pallor of death wound its way up her spine, leaving her feeling isolated and angry. The ripples of this would spread far and wide, destroying the peace she worked hard to maintain.

The Spirit of Chicago solidified a little more, filling in enough space to cast a shadow of his own and whistling the first few bars of 'All I Want For Christmas'.

Delilah sighed and shook off her malaise. "I guess that's our social plans canceled."

"Ours?" the Spirit asked. "My invite to the cookie swap must have been lost in the mail. I was going to make snickerdoodles."

"There's a man dead and you're joking?"

He held up a translucent hand. "Ghost?"

"Who can swim and grab towels?" Delilah raised an eyebrow. "Let's try the truth. You're alive and well but you can phase in and out of places."

It was his turn to shrug. "Physics is not a class I really understood."

Delilah watched the news crews and police for a moment longer before walking away.

The Spirit of Chicago kept pace with her. There were no footprints, something she should have found more disturbing than she did.

"Are we sharing information?" he asked.

"If I find any, I might be persuaded to share. There's no profit in this kind of crime, and I'm vexed beyond words that someone would invade my city like this," Delilah said.

"Yours?"

"I'm very possessive." Delilah hit the call button hidden in the folds of her coat, summoning Freddie.

The Spirit stood beside her, staring up at the sky. "How will I find you?"

"How do you usually find me?"

He eyed her sideways. "I show up at a scene of a crime and you're there waiting for me."

Delilah smiled as the cab pulled up. "Sounds like a plan. I'll see you at the next crime scene, then."

CHAPTER SIX

Dad,

Something's being brokered in Chicago this week. Things have been quiet. Too quiet. And I've been told a hunter's coming to town. I don't know what's going on, or if the mayor's death is related at all.

Help me figure out what I'm looking for, so I can deal with it ASAP?

D

THE SPIRIT OF CHICAGO drifted through the walls of the late mayor's office. Bookshelves lined two of the walls, another was occupied by a window overlooking marble columns to the street below, and the last was covered a detailed map of the city. No personal objects on display; the family photos had come down a few years ago when Mayor Arámbula and his wife had separated.

The Spirit of Chicago reached out and tapped in the security code on the keypad. For a few minutes at least, he was free to look around.

All the books were in their places. They were the first things he remembered. Very early in his career, Arámbula, then a city alderman, had invited him over to see the house. There was a duplicate library. The mayor bought two of every book, one for home and one for the office, so he never had to worry about forgetting something.

People had underestimated Arámbula. He'd been a force of nature, a bombastic man who steamrolled his com-petition and naysayers. He was loud, larger than life—almost immortal.

The Spirit of Chicago frowned as he surveyed the room. Everything was eerily normal. He half expected Arámbula to come charging down the hall like a small locomotive, bellowing rage as he shook one of the increasingly rare print editions of the Chicago daily paper.

The police were going to pin the murder on either family trouble or political enemies, but that didn't feel right. Arámbula was rumored to be involved in half a dozen scandals on any given day, but The Spirit of Chicago knew he wasn't. And the divorce had been amicable. Elsa had a new husband, and Arámbula had walked her down the aisle. Privately, he told his friends he was hunting for someone a little younger. A mid-life crisis wife. It was his idea of a joke.

The Spirit of Chicago nudged the curtains aside, not willing to risk turning on a light that could be seen from the streets outside. Moonlight spilled through the clouds and glittered on a golden apple.

That was new.

The Spirit of Chicago picked it up. Arámbula was not a man who invested in paperweights, and an apple wouldn't have been his style at all. A recreation of a Mycenaean bull statue, yes. But an apple? Apples were for teachers, a moniker no one would have dared use for Arámbula. The Spirit picked the apple up, peering at the smooth surface for an engraving, some hint of where it had come from. The moonlight fractured oddly as he turned it. So many angles. Almost like... He tilted his head and saw a number in the pattern: seventy-seven.

* * *

Delilah growled under her breath and switched the police radio off. All the chatter about the morning commute was distracting her. So, Arámbula was dead. That left a power vacuum at the top of two food chains.

She grabbed Alan Adale's file from her desk. File folders were dinosaurs, and the office staff loved teasing her about her manila addiction, but there were advantages. No one could hack a paper file. No one could search her hard drive and find a copy of this information.

Not that she had much about Adale that wasn't public knowledge. For all his cold, mafia-man appearance, he had a record cleaner than a priest's miter. Normally she liked men without any obvious vices, but this one was getting annoying. Especially since she couldn't seem to give him no as an answer.

There was a shortage of perfect men in the world. Adale was attractive, intelligent... If she compared him to a list of qualities she wanted in a long-term partner, he looked like a winner. But the relationship had one fatal flaw: she didn't want to know what he honestly thought of her. Honesty was the death of infatuation.

"I need a social life," she muttered with a sigh.

"What?" Travys said, freezing in the doorway, his arms once again full of boxes. Luckily for him, one of those boxes was donuts.

"You brought me breakfast?" Delilah asked as she took the donuts and set them on her desk beside a stack of manila folders.

He shucked his bulky winter coat and kicked it carelessly under the chair. Such a boy thing to do. "Hungry bosses are mean bosses."

Delilah smiled and peeked inside. "Boston creams! Now I know you want something. What is it?" She picked up the chocolate-covered pastry and bit in.

"I have a Christmas wish list." His eyebrows bounced up and down in a hysterical attempt at an eyebrow waggle.

"Mmm?"

"Well, I was thinking, since I'm spending Christmas alone—"

"You're not spending it alone!" Delilah huffed around a mouthful of donut in annoyance. "We're doing a family Christmas in Vermont, New England's Winter Playground. I've already rented the house."

Travys looked at her in confusion. "Who is doing a family Christmas?"

"All of us. Angela, Ty, Aaron, Maria, Blessing, Gideon, Mom and Dad of course, you, me, most the minions will be up there. You know, the family."

He picked his own donut out of the box. "At this point we probably need to start putting a capital F on Family."

"Daddy is not the Godfather type."

"Are you sure he's not still trying to take over the world?" Travys asked, his eyes narrowing with suspicion.

Delilah shook her head. "We convinced him to settle for a fiefdom. He has the castle and we own most of Llano County now. It's enough, I think. I mean, taking over the planet in one generation is a pretty ambitious project, and he's retired."

"From being a super villain," Travys said.

"Exactly. His activities are strictly legal right now." She finished her donut and guiltily added, "Ninety percent of the time. Probably. Maybe more like sixty. Still. He's getting better."

Travys rolled his eyes.

Delilah sighed. "Never mind. You're coming with us. Christmas is handled."

"And how am I supposed to get gifts for everyone?" Travys demanded. "Aaron's got his brother's bank account. Gideon has his own company. Am I supposed to go shopping with my intern salary? What's that gonna buy?"

"Do you never check your emails?" Delilah shot back. "Everyone was given a name and twenty dollar gift limit. Trust me. You'll be fine."

"Twenty bucks?" Travys sat down with a frown. "So that's a no to my new car for Christmas?"

"Maybe for graduation." Delilah patted him on the head and turned back to her white board filled with purple ink and power struggles. "I need a pattern to emerge. Does the oracle of Delphi have anything for me?"

Travys shook his head. "Nothing." He closed his eyes. "I can give you a solid bet on who the next mayor will be."

Delilah waved a dismissive hand. "Alan Adale. He's politically hot right now, the press loves him, the people are enamored with him."

"Which is why you're not dating him?" Travys guessed.

She arched an eyebrow. "Adale has every red flag for a user: bad childhood, no significant relationships, and too much money to care about people."

"Have you ever considered that he's maybe not a bad guy?" Travys asked. "It's possible to be devastatingly handsome, have a bad childhood, and still be amazing."

Delilah gave him a look.

He held up his hands in defense. "All I'm saying is that I have red flags all up in my background and you gave me a chance."

"Stop using logic and reason on me. My mind's made up." She uncapped her white board marker with a click. "Help me find my killer. Adale is the best suspect—"

"But he was at the party last night," Travys said.

"Could be a well-planned alibi." She shrugged. "But anyway, I don't think Adale is the killer. I think he's the next victim."

Travys frowned at her. "You getting premonitions now?"

A whisper of ice slid down her spine as she remembered Ivan's words at the party. "No. Just something a little bird told me. Chicago's become ground zero for a hunter who likes big prey."

Travys's eyes widened. "I really hope you mean street rats."

She shook her head. "Serial killers."

"Plural?"

"If my source is accurate, yes. The thing is, they like to know their victims first. Buddy up and give them the choice to join or die."

"Arámbula must have said no."

Delilah rocked back in her chair. "Let's get the mayor's phone records. Then get Adale's, and see if we can tap the police street cams and find him. I want to make a timeline for him from, oh, let's say first of November through whenever we finish this project. Phones, schedule, witnesses, bank accounts. It'll be a fun little side project for you."

Travys gave her a skeptical frown. "Superheroes on TV are way more exciting. No one sits in front of white boards in the movies."

"Sue for false advertising," Delilah advised.

Travys glared at the board. "You sure it was a serial killer?"

"Not yet, but I'm sure we'll find out—" A buzz from the front office interrupted her. Delilah nodded, and Travys hit the button on her desk for her. "Yes?"

"Miss Samson, Detective Morrow of the Chicago PD is here. Are you with a client?" Margo the secretary asked.

"No, I'm free. Please show him back."

Travys raised his eyebrows questioningly.

She shrugged with a frown. "I've got airtight alibis for everything."

"I bet." He stood up and grabbed the files. "I'll go start that file on the deputy mayor."

Delilah opened the door for him. "What else is there to do, right?"

"I have my mom's file. There's a business card in the box that I thought might be a lead." The box was still sitting by the donuts.

"I'll look at it after I talk with the police. Promise."

"Thanks." Travys hurried down the hall, nodding to the gruff police officer coming the other way.

Delilah stayed by the door as she waved the policeman into her office. "Detective Morrow, always a pleasure to see you. Although I doubt you're here for fun."

"I wish," Morrow said. He took his hat off, but remained standing. "This is, officially, a social visit. I came by to invite you and Wil to the annual benefit dinner we're having next week."

Delilah returned to her seat, hiding her internal turmoil and boiling curiosity. "Unofficially?"

"Wil says you sometimes do side projects."

Her pulse skipped. "We all do. A little light body guarding, fieldwork for bonuses. It's all above the board."

Morrow pulled a video stick from his pocket and flipped through the pictures before holding it out to her. "Images from the mayor's office taken this morning by the forensic crew. Notice his desk?"

"Everything seems normal." She touched the screen and zoomed in. "You guys need better equipment."

"We got new stuff last year. Every picture in the office came out distorted until we took the apple out."

She froze. "Apple?" Serial killers with an apple as a calling card. She knew who that was right away, and none of it was good.

"A golden apple paperweight. We think it's bugged, but our tech people haven't figured out how it works yet. They're trying to crack it open."

Delilah was already shaking her head. "Bad idea. Don't do that. They tend to explode."

Morrow let out a breath she hadn't realized he was holding. "Yeah. I'd heard about that. In Atlanta, right? After the DEA officer was shot?"

Delilah exhaled, rubbing at her forehead. "Last October. This spring the Wooden Wonder had an apple on him when he was killed." She met Morrow's eye. "Apples are not a good thing. Though the warped images is a new twist," she added.

He perched on the edge of the spare seat. "What information can you give me?"

"Lots of guesses and no names, alas." Delilah tapped the video stick in her hand. "The apples are the calling card of a serial killer, or group of serial killers, who call themselves The Golden Hunt of Atlanta. Possibly a reference to the city, possibly a reference to the mythical Atlanta. I think they started as a normal hunt club, going after deer and foxes, but someone at the top isn't right in the head."

She stared at her white board, the hastily written names blurring into abstract art. "They started hunting humans. Picking off the weak, the forgotten. They prey on the most vulnerable."

"Like wolves?"

"Like vultures." Rage simmered beneath her calm facade. One day she was going to find the leader of the Hunt, and then God have mercy on his soul, because she wouldn't. "I've linked nearly twenty deaths to the group. Some of the kills are straightforward, like Arámbula. The more dangerous they consider the victim, the more they like to toy with them. The Wooden Wonder was a superhero, nigh on immortal as we would understand it. Almost nothing could hurt him, but they burned him alive."

Morrow had settled back in the chair and was taking notes. "Why? What's the motive?"

She stared at him, eyes cold. "Survival of the fittest, detective. They are Darwinists. Except they take it to an extreme only Hitler could appreciate. They believe they are superior, and the rest of us are just animals. We're prey." Delilah smiled, but she knew it didn't soften her features. "I have a transcription from the one caught in the DEA case." She pulled it up on the computer.

"Did the guy go to jail?"

"He died three hours after booking. The arresting police officer died in a traffic accident the same night."

Morrow frowned at her. "How'd you get a copy of the interrogation?"

She shrugged. "My tip led to the arrest, and I was with Officer Kimley when it happened. Out of habit, my recorder was on. I wanted evidence for court. Emmet Grear babbled like a brook. He told us all sorts of things, some of it utter nonsense, but the Atlanta PD couldn't take the case any further. The perpetrator was dead."

"But he had someone on the outside," Morrow argued. "He had someone mess with Kimley's car. Right?"

"That's always been my suspicion, but I could never collect enough evidence to move on it. They're cagey. They like anonymity. The apple is for the victim. They want them to know they're about to die. They want them to run scared."

Morrow shook his head. "That's just sick."

"It's a troubled world, detective." She held his video stick out. "I'll send you all the files I have."

"Send it to Gelphi, he's handling the investigation."

"Are you sure you don't want copies?"

Morrow pulled his hat on. "Officially, no."

"I'll send the files to your private email then," Delilah said, softening to a real smile. "Along with a question about the dress code for the benefit dinner."

He winked at her. "You're the best. Don't let anyone tell you otherwise."

"I never will."

CHAPTER SEVEN

Dear Maria,

Where the hell is our baby sister? I tried emailing Noah and, lo and behold, his military address no longer works. Did you know he wasn't active duty anymore? I didn't even know you were allowed to quit! You don't think he's in trouble, do you? He would definitely call someone if he was in trouble. He'd call Blessing, right? So where is she?

Call as soon as you can,
Delilah

GOLDEN APPLES. THE SPIRIT of Chicago balanced his chair on two legs and put his feet up on the table. He'd snuck into Chicago's main library after hours to see if the book he remembered from childhood reading forays was still in circulation. It was, and now he was ensconced on the eighth floor of the

Harold Washington Library Center, reading the old mythology book like he was twelve again.

He flipped through the weathered pages, ripped and torn by thousands of careless hands over the years—and repaired with great patience, no doubt. Golden apples. He couldn't shake the feeling that it meant something. There were the Golden Apples of Discord, used by the goddess Eris to start the Trojan War. For Kallisti, the fairest.

Well, he doubted anyone had needed to convince Helen to leave her aging husband for a younger man. That happened even without meddling goddesses. There were golden apples of immortality in several mythologies.

A beguiling idea, but that didn't seem right for a serial killer, not unless he thought killing people would bring him immortality. And there were the golden apples of Atlanta, thrown during a foot race to distract the goddess. That sounded almost right. Distractions...

He shelved the book back where he'd found it and drifted through the library. From his pocket he pulled a page from Arámbula's day planner, the unofficial one no one was supposed to know about. The ripped page had been crumpled in the jacket the mayor had left in the office after the meeting. There was a partial date on the corner.

Three numbers and a hunch wasn't much to go on, but it was a start. He stepped through a wall into the shadows, and out into the snowy Chicago night.

* * *

No one at Sub Rosa Securities knew about Delilah's alter ego, the super-villain-by-default Locke. They'd hired her at the Blackhat conference in Las Vegas when she was still playing around as LockPick and earning good money finding holes in people's security systems. Subrosa offered her all that and healthcare. She'd signed once they added a rider to her contract that kept them from asking too many personal questions about life before they hired her.

During her three years in Chicago, no one had ever questioned her results. Legal methods turned up plenty of dirt; her methods turned up more. But Wil had never once asked why. She was pretty sure he wouldn't believe her anyway, even if she swore on a stack of Bibles.

Still, over the years she'd found fewer and fewer reasons to pull out her steampunk suit with its clocks, copper curls, and a top hat. There were better ways to curb her curiosity. But tonight she needed Locke. She needed to have some-thing for people to look at, if they looked at all, because Kalydon hadn't left traces on the computer.

Three hours of gleaning every grain of information from the web had resulted in a pitiful biography. Edgar Kalydon had been an average son of a blue-collar family until a lottery ticket on his 18th birth-day had changed his life. He'd dropped out of school, found himself an accountant, and enjoyed his life living off the interest.

There was no record of drug abuse, and although he'd gone through four wives in under twenty years and any number of girlfriends, there was no abuse reported. His major vices seemed to be a stubborn self-centeredness—something Delilah didn't find herself quick to condemn—and a passion for hunting. He'd been a big game hunter in his younger years, and an avid skeet shooter well into his sixties. Now, nearly eighty-five, he seemed to have settled down.

Maybe it was paranoia that made him so cagey. Or maybe he was a victim of the hunt too, being stalked like Arámbula had been.

"Hudson? Thames?" Delilah called over her shoulder as she shrugged a Kevlar jacket cut in Edwardian style on. Four points of red light lit the dark hall—eyes, although not the sort most people liked to see. Hudson and Thames were gargoyle-style Minions, genetic marvels created in her father's lab to guard her in the big city. "Fly over to the Wacker building. Do a preliminary scan, and settle down to watch. I want reports coming into base in thirty-second intervals, and instant alerts if Kalydon arrives. Do you have all the information you need?"

There was the sound of stone scrapping against stone as Hudson opened his mouth. "Yes, ma'am."

"Good. I'll be there in twenty minutes." She finished dressing and strode to the control room.

When she had originally bought the apartment, the realtor had waxed poetic on how nice it would be to have a second bedroom, how big it was, what a nice nursery or guest room or workout room it would make. Delilah had nodded noncommittally; the poor woman's nerves wouldn't have handled hearing her real plan, which was to make it a windowless safe room with a super computer that made everything they had at Langley and the Pentagon look slow.

Fortunately, the computer drew power from a kinetic energy strip she'd installed in the subway system and didn't affect her power bill.

Her minion-in-chief glanced up from one of the terminals as she entered. There was no denying that Freddie was a warty, bulbous affront to nature and the good reputation of frogs everywhere, but he passed for a short human in a trench coat and fedora, so she'd never com-plained. "Kalydon left the building ten minutes ago, ma'am."

Delilah nodded. "Is there anyone else on the premises?"

"Two desk clerks sitting in the lobby. They alternate rounds on the main floor every two hours, checking locks and stuff. It's all for show," he said laconically.

She nodded again. "Should be easy enough. What's the angle of entry?"

"Building across the street. Subrosa has security there." He passed her a tablet with the building layout.

"I know this one."

"We can create a window for seven minutes. Long enough for Thames to tie a zipline on, or fly you across."

Delilah scooped up a handful of tiny golden buttons from a bucket near the computer. One of them buzzed. When activated, they were pinky-nail sized bugs capable of flying and attaching themselves to her chosen victim. In the unlikely event that Kalydon had no security in his apartment that would detect them, she'd leave a few of the snoops behind.

"What do normal girls do on a Tuesday night, Freddie?"

"I wouldn't know, ma'am."

"Neither would I. Pull the car around. I'll be down in a moment." With a perfunctory bow he left the room, webbed feet flapping on the tile. Her other minions, all miniatures of Freddie, continued with their work, bat-like ears twitching as they listened to the Minion Midnight radio station that was tuned too high for her to hear.

There was probably something unethical about creating a sentient species and immediately putting them to work for you. Probably. But his lack of ethics was what made Daddy a successful super villain—and she couldn't help but think that it also contributed to his success as university professor when he left his life of crime. Grad students and minions had a lot in common, including, cold, clammy hands.

Delilah shuddered and left the room to check the

mirror one last time. The trick to an effective disguise was to wear something that could pass as commonplace without being everyday wear. The steampunk community in Chicago was legendary, ever since the Affair of 2017. Teenagers wore gear-worked backpacks to school, painted their nails rustic copper colors, and read H.G. Wells on e-readers covered in Gail Carriger stickers.

Most nights of the week it wasn't uncommon to see groups of 'punkers traveling around, usually en route to their role-playing guilds. Even in the dead of winter they were out.

Delilah's outfit blended in with them: a heavy, black-wool coat with brass buttons, a top hat with gears and turkey feathers, and a Daddy-modified pocket watch that was probably breaking the Geneva Convention just by existing. The corset was something she'd picked up at a Ren Fest, along with the leather britches. The boots were from a thrift store, and the copper curls were from her metal-working class in high school. Her teacher had been less than thrilled with the sharp-edged wig, and after some thought, Delilah had rounded the edges so she didn't slice her throat open tossing her hair.

Satisfied that she could pass as just another disaffected college student rebelling against the social norm, Delilah headed downstairs. Freddie was waiting in the underground parking garage in her cab. "Seventy-Seven Wacker, please, Freddie. There's work to be done."

CHAPTER EIGHT

Dear Blessing,

I have a ticket for a flight out of O.R. Tambo Inter-national in Jo-burg for the twentieth. If you can't get to South Africa in time, let me know, and I'll send a charter flight to anywhere but a warzone. I know you loathe checking your email, but please, respond!

If it helps at all, Noah is stateside again. The house we're renting for the holidays is less than an hour from his parents' place.

Totally bribing you,
Delilah

INSIDE 77 WACKER, DELILAH leaned against Kalydon's apartment door. The old wood was cold and smooth beneath her fingers. She let out a breath and a part of her travelled with it, seeping into wall

and the wood, flowing between the molecules, searching for the break between the wall and the door.

Theoretically she could simply break the bonds
between the molecules in the wall and make her own
entrance, but that was always a tricky proposition.
She'd tried it once or twice, at home in Texas where
large explosions went un-noticed by the cattle and
jackrabbits. Molecular bonds packed a lot more energy than a twelve-year-old could anticipate though,
and she'd accidentally burned a large hole in the Hill
Country trying to take a tennis ball apart. Over the
years she'd learned to control the energy release, take
it into herself or displace it somewhere nearby, but it
still tended to be messy.

Delilah's senses crept outwards. A line of metal
divided the wood of the door from the wall, but that
was it. No real door—and absolutely no lock to pick.

In the corner of her vision, something moved.
Delilah pivoted, looking across the hall at the dark,
blank windows. Forty-eight floors up with no ledges,
and no escape. She touched her earpiece. "How are
things outside?"

"All quiet," Hudson reported.

"Nothing to see," Thames agreed.

Freddie cleared his throat. "Control has Kalydon
in the building, but no eyes on."

Delilah shook her head. "Not good enough. I want
eyes on Kalydon right now."

"Tricky," said a lighter alto voice that was one of
the gem-series minions in the control room. "The

theater has live security, and isn't readily hackable."

"So send in the pixies."

Various minions swore in a mixture of French and Spanish. The pixies had been made for her youngest sister, Blessing. If you combined reptiles, dragonflies, carnivorous plants, and pure hatred into a flying nightmare, you got a minion who was short-lived, loyal, and perfect for aerial patrol in places where no one noticed three-inch flittering bugs. Her father often referred to them as one of his greatest laboratory disasters, right after the sea monkeys.

Delilah sighed. "Remember—" A scream from the control room cut her off. "...They bite."

"They squish very easily, too," one of the gems said. "Six pixies now en route to the theater."

"Ma'am, there's someone in that hall with you," Hudson said. "I see a shadow."

"No one's come in or out of the building. Front lobby is clear. Both guards are on post," Freddie reported.

At the very edge of her peripheral vision she caught sight of the intruder, a smear of black against the dark windows. Someone started whistling.

Delilah bowed her head and smiled, pulse settling. "Are you whistling 'Hey There Delilah'?"

The Spirit of Chicago swirled closer, becoming almost human. Insubstantial arms wrapped around her waist. "That is your name, isn't it?" he whispered in her ear.

"I can neither confirm nor deny that rumor." She tucked her chin down to hide the smile.

"What are you doing this evening?"

"A little light breaking and entering. You?"

The Spirit of Chicago released her. He seemed solid, although she knew her hand would pass through him like smoke. "A little light prevention of theft and crime."

"I'm not committing a crime."

"Yet."

Pulling a glove off, she fished a piece of paper out of her pocket. "I thought this conversation might come up."

The Spirit of Chicago picked the to-do list from her hand. "Let's see... Pick lock for apartment seven. You know, I'm not a lawyer, but this is something that might be considered incriminating evidence in court."

"That's only a concern if I'm arrested," she said, "and I notice that you left your handcuffs at home."

"Locked to my bed," he said off-handedly.

"Dirty boy."

He leaned against the wall next to the door. "Item two, seduce a superhero. Ah, now I see the problem."

She leaned closer to the door, trying to find the missing lock. Something was barring her way and none of her senses could pick it up.

He winked at her. "You're doing this backward. Why don't you start with seducing the superhero?"

"Because I made the list by priority. I can't jump around higgledy-piggledy. There needs to be some structure." She gave up on the lock. "Are rocket launchers legal in this city?"

"No."

"Do you think you could change that?"

"No."

Locke scowled. "Some date you are."

"This isn't a date. I'm catching you in the process of breaking and entering."

"I haven't broken or entered anything," she grumbled.

He shook the list at her. "Why don't you seduce the superhero first, and then I won't need to arrest you for anything, because you won't be doing anything illegal."

Delilah quirked an eyebrow. "Seducing you is only important if I need to distract you. Which, at this juncture, I don't."

"So unlock the door and kiss me so we can get on with our evening."

She ran her hands along the door again. "Therein you have found the crux of my problem. There isn't a door here."

"What's this?" One barely-solid hand shook the door handle.

"A false door." She eyed the Spirit speculatively. "What's on the other side?"

The glimmer of green light that made up his eyes

winked off and on, his version of a blink. "How should I know?"

"Because it's dark in there and you can go in?"

"That would be breaking and entering, the thing I came here to prevent you from doing."

"So?"

"So, no. I won't go in there without an invitation. Not unless you have proof that there's something illegal behind these walls."

Delilah glared at the Shadow to no effect. "I bet you we'll find some if we go in there."

"And then, maybe, I'll help you. Not before." His hand, warm, solid, covered in a black glove, encircled her wrist. "Let's leave. We don't need to be here."

"We have movement on the elevator," Control reported as she stumbled into the wall.

She tried to shake the Shadow loose, but his grip only tightened. "Control, repeat that. Who came into the lobby?"

"No one," Freddie said. "All known entrances are quiet. Neither of the guards have moved."

She looked up at her gray-faced captor. "Did you bring someone as back up?"

He shook his head. "You have a sidekick?"

"Minions. Super villains get minions. Superheroes get plucky sidekicks."

"I don't have a side kick and you have minions and an intern," he muttered as the elevator dinged. "That's not fair."

Not good. Not good at all. She licked her lips and hoped she had enough of the family charm to talk her way out of this. "Listen, if anyone asks, this is a costume."

"What?"

Delilah was already walking towards the service elevator and the back door. She punched the lift button and hummed tunelessly as she waited for her exit. Beside her the glass windows reflected frosty light. Tempting, but she was too far up and too unprepared for that kind of exit.

The Spirit of Chicago followed her. "What's going on?"

She turned back as an elevator dinged its arrival and the doors opened. A figure swept out in a heavy, black trench coat. There was an inarticulate squawk as if the sound came through water. The man had a gun. Damn! Damn! Sick with fright, her arms leaden with shock, she grabbed for her watch. Too late. And then the Spirit of Chicago was there, standing in front of her like a smokescreen.

Delilah focused her energy on the pocket watch, praying to whatever god cared for small-time crooks that the magnetic shield would protect them both.

It didn't.

The bullet slammed into the all-too-solid shadow and he fell, his weight pushing her into the elevator. The attacker fired a second round. The bullet splintered the doorframe as she hit the button to close the door.

"Freddie, get a lock on my position and pick me up. I have..." She examined the very-human superhero lying in the elevator beside her. She rubbed her forehead. "We need to get to the hospital."

The cab pulled up in a splash of slush as Delilah opened the delivery door and carried The Spirit of Chicago out over her shoulders. "Get this scene cleaned up. No blood. No tracks," Delilah ordered Thames, who stepped out of the car to help her load the fallen hero. "Freddie. I need you in the back with me."

Hudson climbed into the front seat as Freddie scram-bled into the back. "River or hospital?"

Delilah doubled checked the Spirit's pulse. "Hospital, he's still breathing." For now. "Stupid man decided he was going to rescue the damsel in distress." She took her hat and wig off, tossing them into the front passenger seat. "Go dark, Hudson, I don't want anyone harassing the cab companies trying to find us after we drop him off." She gulped down another ragged breath and tried to will her heart to stop racing.

So, she'd almost been shot. No big deal. It hap-pened. She'd survived close encounters before.

But never with casualties after. Victimless crime. Stealing from thieves. Never delivering more bodies to the morgue.

"Are you all right?" Freddie asked.

She nodded, shoving the fear aside. "I hate to be cliché, but who was that masked man upstairs? Did we stumble into the Golden Hunt?"

"Control has pixies quartering the building," Freddie assured her. "We're doing everything we can to find him."

Delilah studied the man in the ski mask bleeding across the back seat of her cab. The right side of the Spirit's black shirt was sticky with blood. "Hand me the first aid kit. We need to staunch the bleeding. Do The Company records say if he's fast healer? Can I let him sleep this off in a hotel somewhere?"

Freddie handed her the kit and helped move the Spirit's arms so she could cut away his black polyester suit. "The Company has no record of him being able to form a corporeal body. They also have no known alias, address, or any other information on him. He's a ghost."

"He's a human who lied to The Company," Delilah said as she dug in the kit for scissors. "Ghosts, as a general rule, don't exist. He's probably like Maria, able to make illusions and control light or something. Maybe be in two places at once." She cut his shirt free and winced in sympathy. The bullet had torn a hole in his abdomen.

"It missed the lungs," Freddie said. "He might still live."

"Yeah." She stuffed sterile gauze in the wound and tried to wrap it. "Take his mask off. I want to see who he is."

Freddie tugged at the black ski mask and revealed a blond man with a face that she would have said reminded her of the better Greek gods if he didn't look exactly like Alderman Adale.

"Merde."

Freddie hissed, as close as he ever came to swearing. "This isn't good."

"You're telling me. We can't let him die. Three super-heroes in a year isn't coincidence; it's targeted racial violence."

"Two dead mayors in less than a week is also a noticeable trend."

Delilah touched Adale's face. Still warm, thank all the lucky stars in the firmament, but when she forced his eye open he showed no signs of waking. She shook her head. "Okay. Game plan. We need to create a crime scene outside Adale's apartment." As an afterthought she turned her earpiece on. "Control, did you copy that? Crime scene at Adale's place. I want shots reported to the police. Get someone on the radio, I want to know when the shooting at the Clousson building gets reported and what they say."

"Copy that," Control chittered.

"Freddie, give me your clothes, we need to get Adale dressed as something other than a second-story man. If The Company doesn't know what he is, I want to keep it that way." She'd flirted with Alan Adale. Had he guessed? When he approached her at the Field Museum a few hours ago, had he been trying to tell her he knew? "I can't believe I killed my first date in years."

"He's not dead yet," Freddie said, pulling his jacket closer. "And outing him might prove beneficial for our long range plans in the city."

She held out her hand. "Revealing the pro tem mayor as a super-powered freak is going to throw the city into chaos and make him the target of every big game hunter out there. Atlanta's Golden Hunt is already working in Chicago. For all we know, the shooter was following Alan." That made her stomach leap. What if they had been following him? "I need a background check on Adale finished. Every-one he's talked to. Every meeting. Every hour accounted for. Start a file on the mayor and start cross-referencing everything he did with what Adale was doing. Find all the points of connection."

Her minion-in-chief frowned, bulbous eyes protruding further than usual under feathery eyebrows. "What are you thinking?"

"I'm wondering if Adale wasn't the target all along. Maybe someone knew who he was after dark, and Arám-bula was just collateral."

"It's coincidence," Freddie insisted.

She shook her head. "That was a well-timed encounter. Too well done for my comfort. Now, stop arguing and hand me your pants."

Freddie grumbled under his breath. "Aren't you going to look the other way?"

"What? What are you trying to hide? You're part frog, part plant. You don't even have genitalia!"

"I have modesty!"

She rolled her eyes and faced the window, watching the Christmas lights dance on the snow until she felt Freddie's pants slap on her hand.

"Hand tailored, I'll have you know. Custom made just for me!"

"By a minion we keep at the castle," Delilah shot back as she loosened Adale's belt. "This is so awkward." A hot blush crept up her neck and she giggled. "See, you mentioned modesty and now I feel bad about stripping an unconscious man."

Hudson laughed in the front seat, sounding more like an avalanche. "We're about to kick the guy out bleeding into the snow and you feel bad about seeing his undies?"

She turned to Freddie for help.

He was laughing at her too.

"Shut up! This is not enthusiastic consent! I don't want to... molest him."

"Just shut your eyes," Freddie said. "I'm genderless, no reproductive organs, so I can't molest anyone. Right?"

"Right." She shut her eyes firmly. No peeking allowed.

"What kind of underwear is that?"

Ha! She peeked. "Those are running shorts."

"Fond of black, isn't he."

"Shut up and put the pants on him. And," she said, noticing the bandage was soaking through, "get him some more gauze."

"Someone is going to notice he's stripped and treated. Shouldn't we... You know... Leave him for the doctors?"

"Gauze!" She pulled the soaked dressing away. A hard lump gleamed sullenly in the cab-light. "His body expelled the bullet. That's good, right?"

"Coming up on the hospital," Hudson said. "There's two police cruisers at the ER door and an ambulance unloading."

"Pull up, we'll push him out on the far side so they don't see in. Freddie, you better switch with Hudson when we slow down, we'll need to evade like the very devil was on our tail."

"Ya think?"

"Less snark, more minioning!"

Freddie snorted.

Hudson slowed the car. "Switch... now!"

Freddie threw the door open, helped Delilah shove Alan Adale into the snowdrift, and hopped into the seat Hudson was hastily vacating. They sped off, leaving the alderman bleeding in the dirty snow.

CHAPTER NINE

Dear Daddy,

Freddie says he needs more pants. His measurements are attached. Don't ask. Just... don't ask.

D

BRIGHT SUNLIGHT WAS OBSTRUCTED by the blocky body of Detective Morrow. Alan turned away and tried to make sense of the pain. Machines. Beeping. Squeaking wheels. Nothing he associated with home.

"How are you feeling?" the detective asked.

"Sore. Confused. Um... This is a hospital, isn't it?"

"John H. Stroger Junior," Morrow confirmed.

Alan nodded and instantly regretted it. Bright lights twinkled in his vision, gradually fading to black spots. "Home sweet home. I wonder if the nurse who named me still works downstairs." He blinked the last of the spots away and found Detective Morrow's eyes. "Pertinent question, why am I here?"

"Someone shot you."

"What?"

Morrow sat down beside the hospital bed. "Last night, around eleven thirty, you were shot outside your home."

"Shot? In Chicago? No. No, no-no. We have the lowest incident of gun crime in the country. People do not get—" His words slurred. What was in that IV? "People do not get, shot," he enunciated clearly.

"Uh-huh. How you planning on explaining the bullet hole that ripped your side open?"

Alan looked down at his aching right side. "Um..."

"You were shot." A notebook appeared as if by magic.

"Cute trick."

"I do parties," Morrow said, pulling a pen out of his jacket pocket. "Now, what do you remember about last night?"

A cluttered mess of colors and shapes gabbled for attention in his mind. "There was a"—not a girl, couldn't say girl, that sounded too young—"a woman. At the apartment. We talked." Flirted. Most assuredly flirted. "We talked."

"Do you remember what you talked about?"

Lock picks. "Stuff."

"And did she have a gun?"

"No. No." He shook his head against the pain. "She didn't hurt me." The fragments of the night before started piecing themselves together. Locke in the hall with her steampunk gear. Flirting. An elevator. A man? Probably a man, stepping out of the elevator with a gun. "How did I get here?" he whispered to himself.

Morrow leaned forward. "What?"

"How did I get here?" Alan asked, louder. "I don't remember that part."

The detective cleared his throat and pulled out an electronic file pad. "According to the nine-one-one report, two calls came from your area reporting the sound of gun shots. First call was at nine-twenty-seven, the second at nine-thirty-one. The second caller reported that they saw a gray sedan driving fast down the street. A traffic camera in your neighborhood picked up a gray sedan doing seventy at nine-thirty-three. Indiana plates. We ran it, the car was reported stolen two months ago. No joy there."

"I was kidnapped?" That didn't work. Delilah had no reason to help him. No reason not to expose him.

Not unless their flirtation meant more to her than she was letting on. The drugs were clearing out of his system fast now that he was awake and focusing. "I hate to ask, but what was I wearing when I was brought in?"

"Same thing you wore to the party last night; black slacks, dress shoes, no shirt. Someone took it off and tried to bandage you up. The pants were ripped at the hem."

His eyebrows went up. "Is that the usual MO for an attempted murder? Wouldn't it be easier to let me bleed to death?"

The detective shrugged. "The running hypothesis at the station is that it was a case of mistaken identity. Most of our violent crimes are related to domestic violence now. The girl you were with, she's not married is she?"

"No, not that I'm aware of. No ring or anything." He'd checked the first time they'd met, and every time since. Delilah wasn't Chicago's most eligible bachelorette, but she was in the top ten and making the boys in town work for her attention.

"Can you give me her name so I can check it out, just in case?" Morrow asked.

"Um..." There wasn't a good answer to that. "We aren't... We weren't... This was not..."

Morrow rolled his eyes. "You're a politician, Adale, not a saint. Just spill already."

"She doesn't want to be in the spotlight. We weren't going public with the relationship yet. It's too early. I don't want people harassing her." Close enough to the truth. Probably closer than the truth would sound. But Morrow didn't look like he was buying it. "I'll call her when I get home and see if she'll talk to you."

A familiar face poked around the corner.

Morrow turned and frowned. "Chief Wyte, good to see you." The detective glanced over his shoulder at Alan. "Do you want visitors? He was out in the foyer when I came in this morning."

Alan nodded to the chief of police. "Hello." Wyte had been one of Mayor Arámbula's poker buddies. He was always around when you didn't need him, always subtly putting down the people around him, always ready to schmooze his way into power and money. "Coming to check on the walking wounded?"

"I'm just being neighborly." Wyte patted Morrow on the shoulder as he walked past. "Great job, Detective. Why don't you take a break while I chat to my buddy here?" The snake oil all but dripped off him.

Morrow peered over the chief's shoulder and waited for a nod from Alan before he left. The detective was good people.

"Chief," Alan said, refocusing his attention. "I wasn't expecting you to stop by."

"Really?" Wyte put a hand to his chest as if he were hurt. "Come on, Alan. We've been friends for how long and you didn't think I'd come out to check on you?"

"Have we ever spoken without Arámbula around?"

Wyte sighed. "You wound me. I know you like put on the Man of the People act, but come on, Adale. We're cool, right?"

There was a knock on the door and Alan's side burned when he sucked in his breath.

"Delilah Samson." Wyte moved in like a heat-seeking missile.

The steampunk Locke was nowhere to be seen in the perfection of Chicago style that Delilah wore as her day costume. Her dark hair was pulled up in an elegant twist and her flawless skin was framed by a tailored purple suit so dark it was almost black. He coughed to hide a snarl when Wyte reached for her.

"Chief Wyte," Delilah held out her hand like she expected him to bow and kiss her fingertips. Wyte almost did. That woman could wrap men around her finger like nobody's business. "I heard you were here."

Alan scowled. Delilah's gaze flickered to him and she winked. It was enough.

"What can I do for you, Miss Samson? Name it, and it's yours."

She fluttered her eyelashes, the little coquette. "Can you make rocket launchers legal in this city?"

"Um." Wyte stumbled over the request, but Alan could see the wheels in his head turning as he tried to think of a way to make it happen. "Well..."

Delilah laughed. "I'm teasing! All I need is to borrow a few plain-clothes police officers for Addison's New Year's Eve party."

Alan rolled his eyes. Petty jealousy was not attractive, he told himself firmly. And he wasn't jealous. Delilah flirted with people. She probably did it without thinking. It wasn't her fault Wyte was tripping over her like some under-sexed pimply teen waiting for his first kiss.

"Will you walk me to my car?" Delilah asked the police chief.

"Of course!"

Of course. Alan ground his teeth together.

Delilah hit him with a dazzling smile. "I did bring a little something for you, Adale. A get well card from Sub-rosa Securities."

"Trolling for clients?" Wyte teased as Delilah left a small white envelope on the nightstand beside Alan's bed.

Her smile was deceptively calm when she turned away. "Subrosa has always made the safety of Chicago's prominent citizens a top priority. You can't have your police everywhere, but I can put a team anywhere in this city in under five minutes." The words were innocuous enough, but there was a hard edge to them that offered the promise of swift retaliation if things didn't go her way.

Alan waited until they'd left before he opened the envelope: a generic get-well card and Delilah's business card. On the back, in a careful hand, she'd written, "Do not trust Wyte."

That put a slightly sinister spin to Wyte's visit. And Delilah's. Was she tracking him or the police chief?

A nurse came in with a tray of what he was certain was nourishing but bland food. "How are you feeling today?"

"Fantastic. I could run a marathon," Alan said. "When are they releasing me?"

"After a gunshot?" Her dark eyebrows climbed. "Honey, you ain't going nowhere for at least seventy-two hours. Eat your lunch and get comfy."

Alan smiled politely and took the food. The nurse nodded approval and closed the door behind her.

Nine minutes later, he ghosted out of the room leaving nothing behind but a memory and a plate of rubbery scrambled eggs.

CHAPTER TEN

Daddy,

Thank you for the watch! It's absolutely perfect, and it even matches my new necklace. See you next week.

Lovingly,
Delilah

DELILAH CHECKED HER WATCH, then looked up at the McCormick Tribune YMCA. It wasn't nearly as dingy as she'd anticipated. True, the rows of neat two-story houses were all closing in on their century marks, and the cars parked along the street were not the newest models by any stretch of the imagination, but everything seemed well kept. Christmas lights adorned the trees. Wreaths hung in windows. Wood smoke and snow filled the air with a wintery perfume. All that was missing was a wintery soundtrack and some mistletoe, and she'd be in a bad made-for-TV holiday movie.

"I told you it wasn't the bad end of town," Travys said from the depths of his hoody and jacket. "Perfectly safe."

"Remind me again how I got roped into this," she said as Travys opened the front doors of the YMCA, hot air and the smell of sweat swamping her.

Travys smiled. "I have to do community service as part of my social awareness class. You are here because you need to leave the office occasionally."

"I'm work oriented." There were a million and one things she needed to do tonight, but the minions were still trying to trace the late mayor's last hours. So rather than pacing the apartment and grinding her teeth, she'd come here. To play basketball, because Travys told her she had to.

"You're a workaholic who's going to die of a stress-induced heart attack at thirty if you don't watch it."

"What are you, my mother?"

"Locker room is over there," Travys pointed.

"I see the sign."

He grinned like a shark who'd seen a seal pup. Poor boy. The chance to school his boss on the court was giving him delusions of grandeur. She hadn't played since college, not competitively, but a girl didn't grow up with four active siblings without learning how to play one-on-one every-thing like a demon bent on the conquest of hell. Delilah changed, tightened her shoelaces, and stretched. A little physical activity was good for the soul. Especially— she snickered—if it left her favorite intern trembling in terror whenever she mentioned sports.

The YMCA had multiple courts laid out side by side. Several games of pick up were going on, and in one corner a middle-aged Hispanic woman was coaching a co-ed little league team with polite English and a few earthy curse words in Spanish. The kids were eating it up. One even made a basket.

Very few of the players turned to look at the new girl. Skinny, white, ponytail... Nothing to see here. If Angela the Hollywood starlet had walked in, people would have turned. If it were Maria, with her dark-tan skin and emerald-green eyes, people would have stopped. If Blessing walked in, pale curls framing a face with lavender eyes, people would have gathered around her faster than she could blink. Even Gideon, their baby brother, would have caught someone's attention. But of all the Smith children, Delilah had to admit she was the average one. Average height. Average weight. Average looks. Average everything. Even her super quirks didn't do enough to set her apart from every other brown-haired, brown-eyed human walking the planet—and she took comfort knowing she was part of a vast majority. Stealth was far, far easier when you had a forgettable face.

Only one person acknowledged her, a muscular blond man shooting hoops with some teens on the far side of the gym. Probably another coach. He nodded to her with a smile, and then made a three-point basket.

"Hey," Travys said, dribbling a ball like a Harlem Globetrotter. "Ready to see my Skillz?"

Delilah snorted. "You did not just put a Z on the end of that."

He laughed and tried to run past her for a lay-up.

Delilah stole the ball, pivoted, and made a basket. "Oh, wait," she said, cocking her head. "Who took her college team to conference championships? Was that me? It was, wasn't it?"

Travys looked at her in mock outrage. "Oh, no. No, this is not happening. I'm young and viral."

"Virile," she corrected as he made a shot, and it boun-ced off the rim. "Okay, maybe viral."

They played a quick game that Delilah won by a point before the group across the gym broke up. "I gotta check in with my people," Travys said.

Delilah raised an eyebrow. "You have people?"

"Quinton. He's a good kid. I'm sort of mentoring him. The Y has a tutoring program, and I'm helping him with math."

"You dragged me away from work to play basket-ball so we could check that this kid is doing his homework?" She rolled her eyes. "I have minions for chores like that."

Travys's wide grin returned. "Yeah, so do I. You."

She wagged her finger at him. "You are getting coal for Christmas!"

Travys laughed at her anger and pointed out a scrawny kid badly in need of new sneakers and a couple of 2000-calorie cheeseburgers. He was... maybe a size twelve mens? Maybe thirteen. She'd have to get Travys to steal one of his sneakers so she could get the size and replace those shoes.

"I need to cut him out of the herd," Travys said. "Isolate him."

"I'm glad you've been paying attention in biology class."

Travys bumped her with his elbow. "Go be my distrac-tion."

"What?"

"Go flirt with his coach or something."

Delilah widened her eyes and pretended to be outraged. "Flirt with a random stranger? What are you, my pimp?"

Travys rolled his eyes. "Just go in and do your girly thing with his coach, so I can get Quinton alone. Please?"

Delilah's eyes narrowed. "What 'Girly Thing'?"

"You know, the flippy-hair pretty-girl thing you do right before you emotionally disembowel people and leave them socially dead. You do it at parties all the time."

"I don't emotionally disembowel people!" Delilah protested as Travys pushed her toward the other side of the gym. "I just speak my mind."

"Trust me, it's the same thing."

Delilah stopped walking when the coach turned. "Alder-man Adale." She looked over her shoulder at Travys who made a shooing motion and then pretended to ignore her. Some days, the universe really was against you. She turned back to Adale. "Hello."

"Hello." Adale smiled.

Quinton shuffled at the alderman's side as Delilah debated what to do. Well, what the hell. Why not? She smiled perkily and tilted her head. "Hi! I'm a distraction! Want to shoot some hoops?" She grabbed Adale's arm and led him away from Quinton so Travys could go in for the kill.

"A distraction?" Adale asked. "What are you distracting me from?"

She fluttered her eyelashes exaggeratedly. "I'm supposed to leave Quinton isolated, so his math tutor can talk to him. I'm not sure if Travys is issuing death threats or trying to convince Quinton that a higher GPA is the only way to meet the University of Chicago cheerleaders. We're supposed to act like we're interested in talking to each other," she added when Adale turned back to the boys with a frown.

"Right, of course." His smile was warm. "How are you?"

"Better than you are, I imagine. How's your side?"

He gave a one-shouldered shrug. "I've been worse. Want to kiss and make it better? Or are you going steady with Wyte now?"

She laughed. "What is this, high school?" She bounced the ball before adding more seriously, "I have reasons to be cautious around Wyte, as do you. Leaving him alone with you while you were wounded seemed like a bad idea."

"So you rushed to my rescue?" Alan teased.

It shouldn't have been funny, but Delilah laughed at the absurdity of the thought anyway. "I hardly think of it as rushing to your rescue after you took a bullet for me. How are you really? Should you be playing basketball a day after being shot?"

"By the time the hospital triage team got to me I was only grazed."

Delilah relaxed. "Here's to fast healing."

Alan caught her hands with a gentle touch and finessed the ball from her grip. "Want to play a quick game of twenty-one while your intern practices his Spanish Inquisition routine on my boy? I promised Quinton's mom he'd be ready to leave by ten."

"He'll survive," Delilah said as she circled around, waiting for an opportunity to steal the ball back. Hot or not, no man who'd just walked out of the hospital was beating her on the court. She feinted in for the ball but Alan twisted, leaving her nothing to do but slap his hip.

"Are we playing or not?"

Delilah raised her eyebrows. "Half-court, poison points at eleven, no tips, no free throws?" They'd shoot only at one basket, each player trying to make twenty-one points with a combination of two-point and three-point shots. Eleven was the poison point; if a player had eleven points and missed their next shot, they reset to zero.

"And here I thought my math days were over."

Delilah shrugged. "I'd love to stay longer, but I have plans tonight and I need to drop Pumpkin back at the dorm before I hit the club scene."

Alan dribbled the ball. "I'm telling Travys you called him a Pumpkin." He feinted left, pivoted right, and still came up against Delilah blocking his way to the net.

"Come on, Adale. Aren't you going to show me some moves?"

He stepped back, dribbling as he watched Delilah. This time he drove left; Delilah swiped the ball out of his hands, pivoted, and made a three-point shot.

"Come on," she taunted. "You have to want it."

He caught the ball as it bounced between the nets. "What are we playing for?"

Distraction. "Fun?"

"How about a kiss for the winner?" He shot her smol-dering look that promised hot and dirty things if she wanted them.

Picturing him naked wasn't necessary—she'd gotten a good show last night. "How 'bout you buy me dinner?"

"Winner gets a free dinner?" Alan sounded doubtful.

"I get a free dinner," Delilah clarified, "because I'm going to win."

Alan shook his head, turned, and did a lay-up. "Maybe you'll have to buy me dinner."

Delilah took the ball. "Mmm, hmm." She stepped closer, invading his personal space, keeping eye contact. Alan's eyes widened. She could hear the hitch in his breath as she brushed against him. She smiled, and shot the ball over his head into the net.

Alan caught her around the waist, and her heart raced as her cheeks heated. "That's cheating!"

"No it's not." They were close enough to kiss. Temp-ting. So tempting. She tore herself away from his gaze and stepped back. Shooting him a flirty smile she sent the ball flying over his head. Nothing but net. "Five to two."

He shook his head and retrieved the ball. Ten points flew past for each of them. Alan jumped and grabbed, pivoted, and scored two more points.

"You're not going to hit twenty-one like that." She shot another two-pointer that sailed over his head. "Oh, wait, that puts me ahead! Nineteen to fourteen, me."

Delilah bent over to pick up the ball, making sure Alan got an eyeful of her hind end while she adjusted her tank top. A little tug down was all she needed.

His eyes widened when she stood up. "That is cheating."

"What?" She batted her eyelids innocently. "A little cleavage wouldn't distract a big, tough politician like you, would it?"

"On anyone else? No. On you? Make a couple baskets already so I can kiss you."

Delilah took an unopposed shot as Alan devoured her with his eyes. "Oh, come on. I know you aren't that tired!"

"I'm recovering from a gunshot!" he protested. "And that was a free throw. One point for you."

"What!"

He smirked as he leaned close to steal the ball. "Twenty to fourteen." Smiling, he shot a three-pointer.

Seven sweaty minutes later Delilah scored her final two points. "I win."

"Right," Alan agreed with a cocky smile. The ball bounced away, forgotten, as he caressed her face. "You win." His lips brushed over hers, warm and tempting.

The list of pros and cons burned to ash at his touch. Love always brought a risk. Relationships brought a risk. But something that felt this good couldn't be wrong, could it? She tilted her head, deepening the kiss. Alan wrapped his arms around her and the kiss became something more, almost desperate. A thousand unspoken words silenced at hundreds of chance meetings fueled their collision.

Movement on the edge of her peripheral vision was the only thing that pulled Delilah away from his embrace. She cleared her throat as Alan wiped lipstick from his mouth. "Well. Hi."

Travys raised his eyebrows. "Hi."

"Are you done?" Delilah asked nonchalantly.

"Am I interrupting something?" Travys asked.

Yes. She made eye contact with Alan. Yes, he'd definitely interrupted something. She just wasn't sure what yet. "I was distracting him. That's what you wanted, wasn't it? Ready to go?"

"Whenever you are," Travys said, frowning at Alan.

"Good night, Alderman." She smiled brightly and walked away, low-grade panic jangling in her chest.

Travys ran to catch up with her. "What was that?"

"I don't know."

"Didn't you say you didn't trust him?" Travys asked, stopping short of chasing after her into the woman's locker room. "I swore that's what you said."

Delilah threw her hands up in frustration. "The situation has changed, okay? I need to go home and think."

Travys let the door swing closed with silent disapproval.

Well, that had not gone as planned. She leaned back against a cold metal locker and stared unseeing at the wall. She had to get that background check finished, it was the only way out of this mess. Either Alan could be trusted, and she was safe to fall in love, or she'd just kissed a man she was destined to kill.

CHAPTER ELEVEN

Dear Maria,

I know you're busy with the elections and everything else that's coming up, but I do need an RSVP for Christmas. It's my year to set up the holiday fun and twist arms. This is Phase One of the arm-twisting. Mom wants everyone home for Christmas. I will beg, bribe, and threaten you with physical pain and the destruction of all you hold dear to make sure you are there.

Let's start with the bribe. I know that in your free time you happened to cross paths with a certain dark-eyed wonder boy who goes by the name of Kon and controls the weather.

I also happen to know that The Company has a very extensive file on him. Sorry, had. Until this morning when I accidentally smashed their firewall to smithereens. The file is now in my possession. And my, but it makes fascinating reading. I may have to give this cowboy a call, see if he likes bareback riding.

Don't even trying to hack my system. The data is on a reserved hard drive and not connected to anything you can touch, kept in an undisclosed location that even my best minions won't divulge.

RSVP or else.

Your evilest sister,
Delilah

ALAN DRIFTED THROUGH THE shadows of the alley to the dead drop, memories of Delilah still keeping him warm. He'd spent all day wondering whether or not he should call her. Twice he'd composed emails. Ads for floral arrangements had teased him, but he wasn't sure if Delilah would like flowers. And, if she did like flowers, she probably wouldn't like them delivered to her office. Peace of mind was out of the question until he could figure out exactly where their relationship was.

Which wasn't going to happen until after this meet-up.

When he'd originally joined The Company, he'd been a distrustful teen who was unwilling to give them too much power over him. Eighteen years of other people picking everything from his name to the food he ate to the clothes he wore had left a mark. He liked the freedom of adulthood, and The Company's standard contract was too restrictive for his liking.

The dead drop had been the compromise. A Company operative left him messages that he'd read and leave untouched in the forgotten space between boarded up buildings. There'd been a dearth of communication since the death of the Wooden Wonder, but last night there'd been a message.

Two women stood under a broken street lamp, one rather elderly with an uptown style and primly pinned gray hair. The other wore a leather catsuit with a slash of red that matched her matte lipstick. Katrina, The Company boss, and the superhero Lead Feather who often acted as Katrina's bodyguard. The Wooden Wonder had once said Lead Feather could kill with a touch, turn people to stone, and stop superpowers from working. It was probably office gossip, but he made a point of avoiding her all the same.

"Katrina." He stayed a shadow, hovering in the darkness out of reach of human touch.

She turned to face him with a scowl. "The Spirit of Chicago? You're exactly how I imagined you."

Lead Feather's fingers flexed in black gloves. "I expected more."

"I'm sorry to disappoint you," Alan lied smoothly. "How may I be of service this evening?"

Katrina glanced at Lead Feather, a sidelong expression she probably didn't intend him to see. "We need to know the city is safe."

"As safe as I can make it."

"And you know of no other mutants here? No rogues or villains?" Katrina asked.

"I've encountered none on my patrols."

"Very good. If you find one, trap them and hold them until we come. The Company has lost too many operatives in recent years. We're to the point where we have to offer even rogues a second chance of safety with us."

"Are fewer mutants being born?" Alan asked.

Again Katrina shared a look with Lead Feather. "We believe so. Super powered humans can't breed. Every experiment and attempt to provide us with another gener-ation has failed. I fear the time will come when you are alone, Spirit of Chicago. The only one who remembers us and our noble purpose."

He and all of Delilah's family, if he'd understood Delilah correctly. "There are rumors of others—"

"We know," Lead Feather cut him off with a snap. "That's why we're here."

Katrina held up her hand for silence. "We're aware of the Russians."

That wasn't what he'd meant, but Alan didn't correct her. Better to leave Delilah's family out of this, though he suspected that if they were anything like Delilah they could take care of themselves. "You want me to follow them?" he guessed. The only Russians in Chicago were not super-anything that he was aware of, but if The Company knew something different, he wanted some skin in the game.

"No," Katrina said. "Tomorrow night you'll come with, unofficially. Once we have the location, I'll place it in the dead drop."

"You can't fight," Lead Feather said in a bored voice. "You can't open doors or repel bullets, but you may be useful in other ways."

"Agreed," he said. "What are we meeting the Russians about?"

"They are rumored to have a black market toxin that is fatal to even our fastest healers," Katrina said, but the way her eyes darted away told him it was a lie. "We need you to watch them. Possibly follow them back to their hide out."

Warning bells sounded in his mind, a sixth sense that something wasn't quite right. "If you wish. I will be as silent as a... ghost." That was essentially the truth. Ghosts were known for rattling around, moaning, and generally causing a raucous when no one wanted them to, and that's exactly what he had in mind.

Fading out of their sight, Alan watched. Curiosity and dead cats and all. There was no logical reason for them not to have an extra person with them unless they were trying to limit witnesses.

"Do you think—" Lead Feather began.

Katrina waved her hand for silence again. "Not here."

They walked nearly a mile of city streets before getting into a plain black four-door sedan. Alan ghosted into the darkness behind the seats, a pool of shadow hidden from sight.

"Do you think the ghost will listen to you?"

"He's not a ghost and I doubt he'll listen entirely, but he's been reasonably good at following directions before," Katrina said as she started the car.

Lead Feather buckled her seatbelt with more force than necessary. "You should have let me take him out. Any super being not under our control is a threat to our existence."

"No," Katrina said. "The ghost is expendable enough, but not yet."

"Do you think Locke will try to recruit him?"

"She's taken others like him. Amber Gris in Maine? That had the thief's fingerprints all over it. And the one in New York last year, the school teacher."

"Rage?" Lead Feather asked. "She only escaped for a few months."

"Long enough to put our operation in jeopardy. We lost Arktos trying to bring her in."

Lead Feather snorted. "He's not lost."

"He's useless if he can't fight or fly."

The superhero snorted in disagreement. "If you thought he was useless, he'd be six-feet under by now."

"He's momentarily useless," Katrina said. "Once we have the Grecian formula we'll be able to bring Arktos back to the fold, and make ten more like him if we want."

Alan slid out of the car; he'd heard enough. He'd always harbored a suspicion that The Company wasn't exactly on the side of angels; this was the confirmation he'd been waiting for. The seller with the Grecian formula was more of a concern. There wasn't an outfit in Chicago that wouldn't like a super powered freak on their pay roll. If he didn't get the drug off the market, Chicago was going to be Ground Zero for World War III.

Brooding, he walked down the dark and empty street to the train station, his body reformed around him. His phone rang. "This is Adale."

"Mayor Adale, this is Chasten Huntley from the office. I was Mayor Arámbula's social secretary," he added in case Alan had forgotten the hyper young man rushing around the office like a fruit fly on a bad dose of meth.

Alan sigh with resignation. "I thought you headed home at five."

"Well, I was, but I came back because I... ah... forgot something and then Mister Kalydon called."

"Kalydon?" Alan searched his memory for the name. "He's an older gentleman, isn't he? Not a native."

"That's him," Huntley said. "He's a major player in the financial sector of Chicago. You probably didn't meet him as an alderman, he's a bit of a recluse, but he's decided to make some time for you."

"How generous of him." Alan rolled his eyes.

"Great, then I'll tell him you'll stop by the club for dinner at eight."

Alan stopped walking and stared at his phone. It was already after six. Factoring in time for dinner, he had less than five hours before he needed to leave for the meet site. "Listen," he said, resuming the conversation. "Tonight isn't going to work for me. Tell Kalydon I appreciate his invitation, but I can't accept. If he's upset, remind him I'm only the temporary mayor. After the voting in January, if I'm elected, I'd be happy to meet him."

"Mister Kalydon is very influential," Chasten wheedled. "I'm sure he could be of great use to the mayor's campaign."

Alan pinched the bridge of his nose. "I'm going to forget you said that. Any meaning would be unethical. I'm not in the business of buying votes."

"S-sorry, sir. Would you, um, be willing to stop by the office again tonight? If you can't meet him for dinner, Mister Kalydon could stop here. Or meet you at your home."

The last thing Alan wanted was a stranger in his apartment. "I'm a couple blocks from the office. If Kalydon can be there in the next twenty minutes, I can meet with him."

"He'll be here, sir. I'll see to it personally."

Alan checked his phone, then turned it off. Kalydon... Kalydon... The name bounced around his head as he walked through the slush to the nearest pedway entrance. Chicago's underground passages, once used for bootlegging, were now the warmest way to move around during the winter. He jogged down the cement stairs to the crowded underground.

An Apple billboard toting the latest in home computer equipment caught his eye. Ah ha. Kalydon was the man who lived at 77 Wacker where Delilah had been scouting, the man Arámbula had gone to meet the night he died.

Alan walked into his empty office twenty minutes later. Everyone was gone for the night except for Chasten Huntley, who was hovering out in the foyer in anticipation of their guest. He'd made a mental note to check into Huntley's background when he had some free time. The boy was way too eager to please, and inferiority complexes were a liability in politics.

Chasten knocked on the doorframe. "In here, sir."

An elderly man followed him into to Alan's Spartan office. Kalydon was an octogenarian who looked a breath away from natural mummification. Wisps of white hair brushed across his liver-spotted scalp. The tatty suit he wore was several decades out of style and sewn for a younger, more muscular, man. He wore rings, thick bands of gold and silver, but nothing else. No glasses, no cane, even though his stride was uneven. His eyes were filled with burning hatred.

"Mr. Kalydon," Alan said, "it's a pleasure to meet you."

Kalydon sat and lifted his chin. "You're a liar. A pretty liar, but still a liar." Chasten stationed himself behind Kalydon, broadcasting his loyalties loudly for those who cared to notice.

Alan nodded. "Right. It's good to know where we all stand. Why are you here, Mr. Kalydon?"

"To see matters settled. I'm moving to Chicago, and I was working with Arámbula to make sure my needs are met."

"I'm sorry, I don't follow. Why do you need the mayor for this?"

Kalydon creaked as he leaned forward. "I have more money than God. I can make you. I can break you. Give me what I want, and we'll be friends."

Alan shook his head. "I'm sorry, what are you looking for? Tax breaks? A license to kill? Introductions to a golf club? I'm very sorry that Arámbula misled you, but that's not what mayors do."

"You can get the superheroes out of my way," Kalydon said. "That'll be enough."

Alan hid his thrill of nerves with a raised eyebrow. "I don't think Chicago has superheroes."

Kalydon sneered at him. "That's what book learning does for you. Makes you think you're smart when you're stupid as a pig. There's at least two in the city right now, maybe more. Monday morning I want you to draft some papers kicking 'em out of the city."

Alan raised an eyebrow. "I'm not Hitler. I won't pin the proverbial Star of David on anyone so you can be happier. And I certainly won't knock on doors to ask people if they're mutant freaks. As long as they're living the laws of the land, I don't care what they do."

"So change the laws," Kalydon said. "Or watch your back. Your choice." He stood up with Chasten's help. "I expect you'll see reason soon enough. If not?" He shrugged. "Politicians are cheap in Chicago."

CHAPTER TWELVE

Delilah,

I'm not going to make it up to surprise Blessing for Christmas like we talked about. There's a mission I need to run. Something last minute. I'm sorry. Tell Blessing I'm sorry. She'll understand. I'll be home by New Years.

Blessing's gift is being mailed to you. Please make sure she gets it on Christmas. Tell her I love her.

Respectfully yours,
MJR Noah Cobb
5 SFG(A), 2nd Battalion
Fort William Henry Harrison, MO
Office: (408) 555-2152

ALAN STOOD IN THE cold, staring at the light shining through his apartment window as snow flurries fell around him. Getting shot had been a very bad idea. Getting shot again because an assassin was waiting in his living room sounded even worse. Two press conferences in twenty-four hours was something that should be banned by the Geneva Convention. And keeping Chasten Huntley on staff was definitely against the eighth amendment. First thing tomorrow he and Chasten were going to have a little chat about acceptable political behavior, and then Chasten could check out with HR and go find a new job. Preferably a long way from Chicago.

But that was a problem for tomorrow.

Frowning, Alan typed in the passcode to get into his building and took the private elevator to the seventh floor. All three of his neighbors were the married-to-work types who saw apartments like this as a place to sleep when in town and nothing more. Alan felt he fit right in.

He unlocked the door and waited for the sound of movement. The light stayed on. Alan pushed the door open and the scent of Chinese food wafted out into the hall.

Delilah sat on the couch reading, legs curled up, high heels lying neglected by the front door. It hurt. The pain of wanting was staggering. How many times had he dreamed of this? Of coming home to something other than a cold, empty house?

Delilah glanced up, smile warm and engaging. "Are you all right?"

No. "Yes."

"You look a little pale."

"Long day at the office." He couldn't seem to convince his feet to move. Everything he wanted was just across the threshold and he couldn't take the step. Delilah stood, long limbs stretching like a ballerina ready to dance. The way her hips moved as she walked toward him was mesmerizing. Every curve begged to be touched. Caressed. And oh, how he wanted to reach out and hold her. But he couldn't.

She stopped in front of him. "Alan? Are you sure you're not hurt?"

"No worse than I was." She took his hand in hers, and the warmth broke the spell. He shook his head. "Sorry. Tired."

"Shock," she said with the authority of one who had seen it before. Delilah tugged at his arm and brought him inside. "Let's sit down and eat."

Alan took his coat off and tried to reorder his thoughts. She wasn't doing this on purpose, he was certain of that. At least, ninety-five percent certain. He'd been on the receiving end of seduction before and it usually involved less clothing on the part of the seducer. One girl had gone as far as to wait for him in his dorm room wearing nothing but a bright blue thong. Delilah was still dressed in her suit from the office.

"Alan?" She laid the plates on the table with efficient ease. "What's wrong?"

"Nothing."

"You're shaking." She came to him, hands brushing his arms. "Are you cold? Sick?" Concern and fear filled her dark eyes. "What happened?"

"Nothing." He stepped away, retreating to the familiar comfort of his overstuffed couch. "It's... silliness. I'll tell you after dinner."

She raised a questioning eyebrow. "It's really hard to partner with someone, or guard them, if they're keeping secrets. I find it particularly annoying." The muscles around her eyes tightened with anger.

He sighed in defeat. "It's been a bad day and to come home to this..." The words trailed off as he choked on the rest.

She sat down across from him. "I didn't think I'd scare you. I didn't even think about how shocking it must be to get shot like that. I'm sorry. That was thoughtless of me." She shook her head in disgust. "You weren't here at eight and I didn't want to sit on the landing while the food grew cold."

"It's not that." He licked his lips as he tried to think of a way to explain. "I'm not good with emotions I guess. It's getting shot, the press conference, Arámbula's viewing, police reports, there was a lot of emotional stress today. Other things. I came home on the defensive. And then you were just here. Sitting here."

"I'm so sorry." Delilah stood up and slipped on her shoes. "Try to eat, please? And I'll, um, send you a text or something if I hear anything about our mutual friend."

Alan spun around in confusion. "What? Where are you going?"

Delilah stood frozen by the hall closet, coat in hand. "Home?"

"I thought we were going to eat dinner together. Catch up. Talk."

"Not when you're already stressed out." She pulled her coat over. With a sweet smile she walked over and kissed him on the forehead, a virgin-saint blessing the sick. "It's not a big deal. This can wait until you recover."

"I'm not stressed!" Alan protested.

"Then what's wrong?"

He sat back, staring at the curtain-covered windows. "I was happy."

Silence filled the room with an unwelcome chill.

"I've never had someone waiting for me. Never had someone care if I was sick, or late, or dead." Old pain stabbed at his heart. "I've never come home to a hot dinner before."

"Well, it's not like it's home cooked or anything," Delilah said with the brittle laugh of someone desperately trying to escape the deep end of the emotional spectrum.

He nodded, still refusing to turn around. A hot meal made him tear up? Very manly. Very romantic. He sighed and waited for the door to creak open as Delilah left.

Her coat flopped over the back of the couch beside him.

"That wasn't a guilt trip," he muttered, vaguely ashamed. "I wasn't trying to make you stay."

"I was going to leave because I thought you needed space." She sat down beside him.

"And now?"

"Now I think you need someone here. To be a friend, if nothing else."

He glanced sideways at her. "What if I wanted more than a friend?"

Her smile turned seductive. "Hmmm." Delilah leaned toward him, hand resting suggestively on his knee. "I'm sure that could be a topic of discussion." Her lips were a breath away from his. "I do have a weakness for brainy blonds."

Alan leaned in to steal a kiss.

Delilah ducked away. "But remember the To Do list. Unlock the door, then seduce the superhero."

"Ah, see, there's our problem. Right now I'm a pro tem mayor, not a superhero. And at the very top of my to-do list is seducing a world-class rogue and security operative."

"Is it?" Delilah gasped with mock surprise, hand covering her delightful lips. "Dear me! Whatever shall I do to protect myself from your wicked blandishments, Mister Adale?"

The thick southern accent she served up made him laugh. "I think Southern belles are supposed to swoon at my dashing and romantic nature and kiss me passionately."

"Really?"

He nodded. "Pretty sure. Read it in a book once."

"Must not have been a Texas southern belle." Delilah stood up, all playfulness gone. "Dinner first. You're still recovering."

"A kiss would make me better."

She arched an eyebrow. "Would it stop with one kiss?"

He paused. "It could."

Delilah didn't seem convinced.

"We should try it. For the sake of science."

She rolled her eyes but came back to him. "For science?"

"Mmmhmm."

"That's your best pick up line?"

"My best pickup line is, 'Hello, what's your name?' But when I used it on you, you gave me a look that promised a painful death and walked away without a backward glance. I remember it quite clearly."

Delilah shrugged. "It'd been a long day and I didn't need another bad boy in my life."

"But I'm not a bad boy," Alan assured her as his hand slipped around her waist to pull her closer.

"You're not a boy at all. I like that in a man."

Delilah's lips were soft, gentle, teasing... like a dream dancing just out of reach of memory. He pulled her closer, wanting to catch hold of the magic she brought with her.

Her fingers caressed his cheekbone. A moment later she was straddling him on the couch and he was lost in her touch.

Delilah pulled away. He whimpered in dismay, and then the whimper became a groan of lust as hot lips trailed kisses up his neck.

"We. Need. To. Eat," she whispered in his ear.

Alan caught her wrist. "Food is overrated."

"If we don't eat, how will we have energy for anything else?"

The promise of more was a drug, a seductive lure with poison inside. Alan narrowed his eyes. "Now you're teasing me."

"Yup," Delilah said as she stood up, pulling him with her.

He shook his head, feeling like a fool. At least that was familiar territory. She wrapped him in knots, played him like a yo-yo, and when she smiled all he could think of was winning another kiss. "You are a wicked, wicked woman, Delilah."

Her eyes sparkled with secret mirth. "Me?" She fluttered her eyelashes innocently. "You seduced me with your suave demeanor and reckless charm."

"Reckless charm?" He propped himself up on one elbow. "If you were enjoying that as much as I was, why are we stopping for dinner?"

"Because you're healing at a superhuman rate, and that takes more energy than you think." She kissed him again, leaving his head spinning. "You're shaking," she said softly. "I stopped because I don't want to see you hurt. Let's eat dinner. Get you healed. And then we'll talk about everything."

* * *

In the study, Delilah held her carton of Chinese food in front of her like a shield to protect her somewhat tarnished virtue. That butt! Alan stretched again, slacks cupping a grade A rump as he rearranged his player board. This wasn't how it was supposed to work. Every storybook said she'd kiss her crush, no sparks would fly, and she'd learn her lesson. It would leave her jaded and better able to focus full time on her work. A kiss to tease the hero wasn't supposed to leave her so hungry for more that Mongolian beef wasn't hot enough to burn away the memory of his touch. She sighed.

Alan turned around. "Are you okay? Am I boring you?"

"Um..." Telling him she'd stopped listening ten minutes ago was going to cause all sorts of problems. "They skimped on the chili flakes," she said, waggling her half-eaten box of dinner. "It's bland."

His lips quirked up in an endearing smile. "I'm so sorry. Do I need to get you some hot sauce?"

Was that a pick-up line? Delilah tried to think of a good reply. I've got your hot sauce right here. I like it hot and saucy, and I'm not talking sriracha.

"And that concludes the boring portion of our evening." Alan coughed and tucked his notes away. "You know all this already, don't you?"

"The board? Yeah, I've got the same one at my place. Great minds and all." She abandoned her dinner on Alan's desk. "The only major difference is here," she tapped Alan's picture off to the side, "here," she tapped her own in the midlevel-hoodlum-management level, "and here," she tapped Ivan's surly mug. "I had you and Arámbula tagged as major criminal players."

"His wife was. Her family is very old, very dirty, and has lots of money."

Delilah nodded. "I figured that out. But I'm still not here, and I think you've got Ivan too high."

"Ivan runs contracts for Vtoraya Volna—Second Wave—they're Russia's answer to The Company, if The Company ran guns for Serbian terrorists. Ivan's American born, Russian raised, and good at not being there when the outhouse hits the fan."

"I noticed that about him."

"He's one of their captains. Not likely to go any higher, but he's not a low level flunky."

She raised an eyebrow. "Which begs the question, 'What is *mon capitaine* doing in Chicago?'"

"Your captain?" Alan gave her a quizzical look. "You and Ivan have a thing?"

"We exchange punches on a regular basis."

"Right. Well, now I'm irrationally jealous of a thug." Alan shook his head in disbelief. "You ditched dinner with me for Ivan."

Delilah laughed. "Not intentionally."

"Uh huh." Alan cornered her against the desk. "You turned me down or canceled every date. How long have I been chasing you? Over a year now?"

"I had perfectly valid reasons." She tossed her hair. "I thought you might get hurt."

"Hurt?" Alan smirked.

Delilah shrugged. "It was a valid concern. If you weren't a superhero you'd still be at the hospital nursing the world's worst stomach cramp."

"So, you're saying I should have led with the superhero thing?"

"Oh yeah." She nodded.

"Because you like superheroes?"

She wrinkled her nose. "I like you. Let's not push any of the other details." She scrutinized the board once more. "Where does Kalydon come into play? He owns the Wacker building. Is he part of this, or no?"

Alan shrugged. "I don't know. Up until today I would have said he's a businessman, older, semi-retired, and all I know from his private life is that he likes hunting. He's a Good 'ol Boy with a chip on his shoulder."

"What changed your mind?"

"He came to my office tonight to make demands. Vague ones. He wants the superheroes out of the city, then said he knows there are two here. He finished by telling me politicians are cheap. I don't know if he meant we were bribable or replaceable."

Delilah frowned at her empty take-out container. "Does he know we're the supers he wants gone?"

"Probably not. He might not even mean us." Alan grimaced. "Which leads to my other piece of bad news for the evening. The Company is in town on a shopping trip."

"They go near Travys and I'll kill them," Delilah said without hesitation.

He shook his head. "No, they're trying to get a formula of some kind. Katrina thinks she can make new super-heroes. I don't even know if it's a real thing though."

"There's nothing like that on the market now, but there's always been rumors. I'll have my research team look into it."

Alan shot her an amused smile. "Research team? Who are you, Bruce Wayne?"

"Mmm, more like Batman's beloved and well-financed daughter."

"Lucky girl." He squared his shoulders. "I'm supposed to meet The Company operatives at midnight. Want to tag along?"

Anything The Company could dish out, she could handle, but it didn't seem like Alan was trying to set her up for a take down. "I have other plans tonight."

"Would I make your life easier if I wrote down the GPS coordinates for the meeting?"

"It would save me some legwork."

He smiled. "Then I'll leave the address somewhere easy for you to find on the way out the door. But, first, is there any chance of a kiss good night?"

CHAPTER THIRTEEN

Dear Mom,

Random question of the day... When you first met Dad, how did you know he was The One? Was there a flash of light? Did he take your breath away? How'd you know he was perfect for you, or was it just a lucky guess?

All my love,
Delilah

DELILAH BALANCED THE TEODORA on one hip as something at her other hip beeped.

"Want help with that?" Alan leaned over her shoulder, arms encircling her as he gently lifted the Teodora out of her grasp. "Now you can answer your phone."

"Give it back." She reached for the gemstone with one hand as she pulled out her phone. "I have a really good reason for taking that home with me."

"Uh huh," Alan said. "Like you have a really good reason for skipping out on our date again? I thought we were meeting to watch the buy."

"I was on my way and remembered I needed to pick something up that I left here after the party."

"A giant emerald?"

She glanced at her phone. A blue light on her phone's map of Chicago showed Travys in the wrong part of town. "I need to get it out before it hatches and eats everything. They're ravenous when they first emerge."

"Hatch?"

"Yes, hatch. It'll eat the other stones, and most of the fossils, and possibly the building. We can leave it at the zoo if you want, but it's not safe to leave here."

"Hatch?"

"What? You thought I actually wanted a twenty-five pound emerald? What would I do with it? Green is not a flattering color on me." Delilah grabbed Alan's wrist and dragged the Spirit after her. "I've got to go get Travys." He slipped through her fingers like smoke.

"What's wrong with Travys?"

She watched the tracking point of his phone. "He's gone and done something stupid."

"You're tracking your intern's phone? Isn't that illegal?"

"It's a family phone." Locks on the cases around them cracked open. Delilah rubbed her forehead, trying to contain her emotions. "Angela is going to kill me."

"Family? What, you're in the mob now?"

Delilah froze halfway down the staircase, where the winter moon threw odd shadows across the darkened museum. "What are you going on about?"

Alan came down the last few steps so he stood on eye-level with her. "You don't look like you belong to a crime family, but..."

"Family; as in Mom, Dad, Brother, Sister. Travys is sort of my adopted baby brother. Sort of. It's weird." She waved his next question away. "Do you know how amoebas roll over and absorb everything they touch? My family is like that. They steam roll and assimilate everything in their path. Travys got caught in it one day, but he's a good kid and he didn't have anyone else, so we dragged him into the clan."

"Why?"

"My sister used to be his math teacher."

Her boots echoed on the tile floor of the atrium and Delilah realized Alan had stopped. "Hello? You have my egg. You need to keep walking."

"You know, I never had a family of my own, but when the other kids in foster care talked about loving home environments they never used terminology better suited for a biology class."

"They probably didn't have a family like mine," Delilah said. "Even by our own lax definitions we're a little weird. Every family is, I imagine."

"I wouldn't know. I never had one."

She pivoted, walking backward so she could watch him. "Did you ever try to look them up?"

He shrugged. "There never seemed to be a reason to."

The lights flickered as the secondary generator cut back in. A siren screamed and she sighed. With a touch of her finger she turned the coms unit on. "Freddie? Meet me at the side entrance. And open the pixie cage."

Alan's footsteps echoed on the floor behind her.

Delilah pulled out her whistle as a voice yelled from the third floor for them to stop. Brightly colored lights flitted past and she barely had enough time to grab Alan's hand as he reached. "Don't touch. They bite."

"What are they?"

"Pixies. Don't ask." She held the door open and shooed him toward the car. "How'd the buy go? Did you see the seller?"

"It was a preliminary meet up with a voice recording on a tape recorder. The thing had to have been forty years old."

Delilah whistled again to call the pixies back before climbing into the vehicle. "And the voice on it was warped?"

"Noticeably." Alan frowned as he pulled his seat belt on. "But I recognized it anyway. Remember Kalydon?"

"The man who said politicians were cheap? Yeah, he sticks out. Freddie?" She tapped the minion on his shoulder as he merged into traffic. "Slow down, or the pixies will never catch up and they'll freeze to death."

The car picked up speed.

"Freddie!" The car slowed and Delilah stripped off her gloves. "Did Kalydon say what he was selling?"

"Whatever it is, he wants one million in unmarked bills and a donor from anyone interested." He shifted the Teodora. "I... just stole this for you, didn't I?"

"Yup."

He closed his eyes. "You are so bad for my moral integrity."

"But a vast improvement to your street cred." She smiled.

Alan didn't smile back.

"It's an egg! Look." She pulled a flashlight from her bag on the cab floor and shone it into the egg. The deep green ribbons rippled, rolled, and two riparian eyes blinked at them. "My father forgot this one when we were on vacation one year. It wasn't incubated at the right temperature and it's only dumb luck the poor little thing didn't die. If it had hatched in the museum there would be all sorts of problems."

Alan dropped the Teodora on the seat between them. "Your father tinkers with a lot of genes, does he?"

"Not officially. He's a professor in ethics. Now." She squirmed. "He was a little bit wild as a kid."

"How wild?"

"America's Most Wanted Super Villain wild?"

Alan seemed to consider this. "I thought the Most Wanted Villain in the world was Strike, and last I checked, she was a woman."

"Is a woman. Yes. My father was a super villain, then he retired. Gave up the life of crime almost completely when he married Mom."

"I feel like I'm missing a story here."

Delilah shook her head. "You have no idea how true that is. Freddie, turn left up here." She turned back to Alan. "Are you coming with me to pick up Travys, or am I dropping you at home? I know you have a city to run in the morning."

"Are you going to need rescuing?"

"That's always a possibility."

* * *

Alan fastened his seat belt and smiled brightly at Locke—she was Locke right now, from her shiny metal curls to the top hat to the thigh-high boots that kept dragging his attention down to where it was not supposed to be. "I'm not leaving."

She rolled her eyes. "Fabulous. Freddie, head after Travys. We don't have time to waste."

"Travys works security with Subrosa. He's probably at a party. You realize that, right?"

Her glare made the wind chill feel warm. "The Company is in town and while Travys isn't going to be a superhero any time soon, he's got enough precognitive powers that he might draw unwanted attention. While there's a threat, he's supposed to stick to routes I have surveillance on. Right now he's out of sight, and I'm worried."

Alan frowned. "I didn't realize he was anything out of the ordinary."

"Most people won't, but that doesn't mean The Company doesn't have someone who can pick him out." Locke shrugged, her copper ringlets tinkling as she moved. "Angela had to protect him. It's really not complicated. If you stay around us long enough, you're either one of us or you're dead. I don't think we know any other way to live. Travys needs people to take care of him, to make sure he's eating right, to..." Her voice trailed off. "Are you all right?"

Belatedly he realized his tightening shoulders had rounded until he was hunched up and folded in the corner like he was three again. "I'm fine."

One eyebrow went up in question. "I can make you tell the truth," Locke threatened.

"I'm fine. It was a stupid reaction." He sighed, forcing himself to relax, and looked out the window at the Christmas lights. "When I was little, that's all I ever wanted: a big family and the postcard-perfect holiday. Candy canes, hot cocoa, sledding down the hill and then running inside to spend time with a huge throng of people who all loved me."

"You never had that." Delilah's voice was flat.

He shrugged. "I was abandoned at the hospital when I was a few hours old. It's not the start of a story that ends with happily ever after."

"You never know," she said as she took off her top hat and wig, once again transforming into Delilah. "Maybe if you're very good, Santa will bring you a family for Christmas."

Smirking, Alan turned back to her. "Right. And what is Santa bringing you?"

Delilah shrugged dismissively. "A pony? I don't know. I don't want things. Anyone can buy things, or, well... Anyone born into a wealthy family like I was can buy things. What I can't buy is safety for my family, or an end to my mother's nightmares. If there was a way to buy that, I would."

Alan leaned forward, interest piqued. "What happened to your mom?"

"She was kidnapped when I was five. The Rainbow Dane had this mad idea that he'd kill all the children of super villains and he was going to get my mom to help because she can move at super-speeds and fly. She wasn't going to, but he used a lotus serum to strip her freewill away. It was rape, but not the physical kind. Everyone thinks she's fine, but people can't lie to me. That's my talent—utterly useless as it is; I can make people tell the truth. So when I caught her crying one day, huddled in the back of her closet during the middle of the day when I was home sick and everyone else was gone, I made her tell me the truth. And she did." Tears sparkled in

Delilah's eyes. "She hates herself. She hates every-thing about herself, because that's what put us at risk. And I can't do a damn thing about it."

"Did you tell anyone?"

"Daddy knows. I think he knew all along. Mom tries to act like it's not a big deal, because the fact that she is getting better is the only thing keeping Daddy in check. But it's going to break down one day. She'll fall apart, because you can't live like that forever, and then Daddy will retaliate and this little cold war we currently have will turn into some-thing that makes World War Two look like a picnic." She pressed her lips together in thought, and then said, "My dad's a little scary when he's angry."

"Good to know." Alan reached for her hand, their fingers entwined. "I'm sorry I brought that all up."

She shrugged. "Someone needs to know, in case I ever go crazy. Keeping secrets... Sometimes it feels like everything is on my shoulders. I know too much to be happy. I know what's wrong with everyone and what they want and why they want it, but I don't know how to fix it."

"That's the secret," he whispered, giving her hand a squeeze. "You don't have to fix everything."

Delilah laughed, light and airy and winsome. "You are definitely not a Smith."

"Your surname is Samson."

"Because I legally changed it at eighteen. I was born Delilah Minerva Sorsha Smith, which is an unholy mouthful with more geek references than any sane person deserves."

"Could be worse," Alan said with a shrug. "I was named after one of Robin's merry men because the nurse on duty that night happened to be watching some old BBC show and thought it was cute. Cute it may be, but it's definitely not modern or stylish."

"Were you teased?"

"Horribly!"

"You would have been teased worse if you were Robin." She flashed him a smile that erased the old pain before turning to the front. "Freddie, how close are we?"

"Another block, ma'am," said the warty thing driving the car.

"Is that what the Teodora is going to hatch into?" Alan murmured.

"Maybe. Possibly." Delilah grimaced. "Honestly, I haven't a clue. Daddy likes to tinker with things. You never know exactly what you're going to get."

The car slowed outside a gated community. "I believe the young gentleman is inside, ma'am. Would you like to go through the gate?"

"No, circle the neighborhood once and we'll find a place to get out. Why a gated community? I was expecting an abandoned warehouse or a brickyard. Something a little more traditional."

Alan frowned at the cookie-cutter houses, all neatly lined up behind shoveled sidewalks. "Maybe he's meeting a friend."

"Maybe he's doing some after-hours snooping. Freddie, stop by those bushes," Delilah ordered. "And get a team working on those gates. I want electricity cut in five minutes." She picked up her phone. "Let's go hunting."

CHAPTER FOURTEEN

SOS - D

DELILAH CURSED THE SNOW under her breath. They were going to leave a trail a blind hamster could follow.

"Where are we going?" Alan whispered in her ear. In his shadow form there wasn't even a hint of warmth behind her.

"See the pretty blue dot on my phone? I'm trying to figure out where the pretty blue dot is in relation to all these over-priced homes. Tacky, turn-of-the-century cookie-cutter homes in a gated community. It makes me weep for humanity. Ugly, ugly architecture."

"Do you always critique your surroundings like this?"

"Yes, it's one of my many failings."

Gentle arms wrapped around her. "Hold on, I think I know where your pretty blue dot is."

Shadows swallowed her as the air turned frigid. Her heartbeat echoed in her ears, and then they were standing beside a house with plastic siding. "Why didn't we go inside?"

"They don't have any shadows. That's why I picked it. Who else would light up every corner of their home?"

She glared up at the windows covered by curtains. "I don't see any light."

"The windows don't go inside the house, they're built into a layer of the wall, like a safe house."

"Charming. For the record, I don't approve." She tapped a fingertip against her chin.

"I didn't think you would."

They stalked around the corner, quietly opening a chain link fence to sneak into the backyard. "It looks so normal." Snow, dead branches sticking up like the skeletons of spring, the winter perfume of wood smoke and... Delilah inhaled deeply. "Do you smell lotus flowers?"

"I don't even know what they smell like."

She inhaled again. Under the scent of wood smoke was a hint of rain forest, sweet and a little fruity with the promise of jungles and exotic locales. Definitely not the usual scent associated with Chicago suburbs in the dead of winter. "It's like orange blossom. You don't smell it?"

Alan shook his shadowy head.

"I hope I'm wrong. The Company hasn't started

using chemicals to control their super-slaves, have they?"

"And I would know that how, exactly?" he whispered as she approached the back door.

She took off her glove and gripped the cold metal as she tried to reach the lock. But like Kalydon's apartment, there was nothing there.

"Problems?"

"Too many to count. This isn't an entrance."

"Probably fake like the windows."

"And there are no shadows inside?"

"Not unless you want to appear inside someone's clothing."

"How many people are in there?"

He closed his glowing green eyes and his lips moved. "Six? Maybe seven. Counting the shadows inside clothes is not an exact science."

"None of them are on this end of the house, are they?"

"All the small shadows are in the basement."

"Fine." She released her power. The metal door-knob shook under hand, burning and melting before the door exploded with a sound that made her ear-drums sore. "Knock, knock?"

She stepped into a stripped room with bright photography lights hanging every few feet, planted in the walls, strapped to every corner. "I guess they knew you might be in town."

"Looks like."

Voices filtered through the house's cold air. Delilah followed them, anger growing as the smell of lotus blossoms became ever more distinct. Damn them all to the seventh hell. If they'd poisoned Travys the way the Rainbow Dane had poisoned her mother, she'd see them all burn. The basement door exploded before she even touched it.

"Calm down," Alan whispered in her ear. "You can't kill them."

"Yes, I can," she bit off as the stairs shuddered under her steps.

"Okay, but you shouldn't kill them."

The door at the bottom of the stairs was heavy and metallic. "That has yet to be determined." The door disintegrated. "Travys?" she called, amazed her voice wasn't shaking. Tears filled her eyes. That smell! That horrible, horrible smell! The one her mother had puked all over the car when they'd driven away from Colorado and the superheroes who'd wanted her family dead. It was etched in her brain with the worst form of emotional acid. "Travys, you find the kinkiest hide outs." She stepped into the basement and saw Travys strapped to a chair and stripped to his tighty-whities. An IV tube hung from his arm, dripping blood onto the floor. "Travys!"

Alan reached him first, removing the IV needle and covering the wound with his solid hand. "Shh," he said. "Do you have a first aid kit?"

She took a shaky breath and nodded.

"Take care of him. There's a tunnel. I'm going to follow them," Alan said.

"Don't get caught."

He turned to a curl of smoke in answer.

She stepped to Travys's side, holding his injured arm with one hand as she dug through her bag. On cue, the lights died. "Control? Do you have me?"

Nothing.

"Travys? Travys, come on. I need you to wake up now." She flicked her flashlight on, put it between her teeth, and bandaged his arm. Travys groaned. "That's a good boy," she said indistinctly around the flashlight, saliva trailing out of her mouth as she tried to talk. "Come on." She held the ropes, letting them unlock in her hands before dropping them in evidence bags. Detective Morrow was going to kill her. This case was one serious SNAFU after another. A known killer, but not enough evidence. Evidence in the form of a kidnapped college student, but she'd ruined it.

Travys's head lolled to the side.

"Hey, hey, come on. I need you to wake up." She checked his pulse; it was slow but steady. Why the hell would anyone want his blood? "Kid, if this is some weird initiation rite for a frat that you forgot to tell me about, you will never hear the end of it. Didn't you ever watch the classics growing up?" she asked the unconscious Travys as she slung him over her shoulders in a fireman's carry. Stumbling through the dark, she found her way to the stairs. "If you'd seen even one episode of Buffy you'd know what a bad idea wandering around town alone is. Or Veronica Mars. I'll make you watch that," she huffed. "You can learn all about the dangers of not communicating with people. Was one phone call too much to ask?"

She sank to her knees half way up the dark stairs. "Hey, Delilah, I'm going to this place. Can you do a background check? And I would have said, 'Why, yes, Travys!' And, 'Don't go, Travys, it's full of vampiric suburbanites.'"

"You talk too much," Travys muttered.

Delilah forced herself up, climbed the last few steps, and rolled him off her shoulders to the floor.

His teeth chattered, but his eyes opened. "Why's it so cold?"

"No one thought to install a heater." She took her coat off and laid it over him. "Stay right there, I'm going to see if I can find anything else upstairs."

Travys lifted his head off the floor. "'Lilah?"

"It's okay. I'll be right back." With a forced smile she headed upstairs, hitting her comms unit. "Hello? Control?"

"Ma'am?"

"Freddie! Lock on to me. Get the car here now. Make a scene. I want the cops crawling all over this place by dawn."

"Yes, ma'am."

The upstairs was much like the downstairs, heavily lit and stripped of everything that might make it homey. No paint on the sheet rock walls, no windows, nothing to indicate that someone had once lived here, although they obviously had. The outside was too tidy to be an abandoned home. Details from the outside filtered back in her mind. She'd seen curtains like that before, a hot cranberry color that was an offense to Mother Nature. Sadly, it was popular this year. So, new curtains and a cut lawn, but a stripped interior. Chicago Tribune's front-page headline for tomorrow was already written.

None of the rooms held anything; even the bathroom was torn down to a faucet and yellowing toilet. On impulse, she went to the attic. There probably wasn't anything but insulation up there, but she'd feel better having checked everywhere.

"Almost to your location, ma'am," Freddie said over her comm. "We'll need to leave in a hurry. The gate guard was less than polite."

"I can't imagine why." She found the attic door and watched it drop to the floor as her powers eased the locks open. "Travys is in the kitchen, go around back and load him into the car. I'm checking the attic. There's a heavy lotus smell." And the dusty attic door reeked of the potent flower. It took two tries for her to jump high enough to grab the rim of the attic opening and pull herself up.

As she'd expected, the attic was lit with the same heavy-duty lamps found throughout the house. It seemed like a huge investment just to keep the Spirit of Chicago at bay. Why not pick a smaller house to use if you were going to light it up like this? Why do it at all? There had to be better things to do with your life. Delilah walked the perimeter of the attic, stopping where the window should have been. Nothing. Time to go, then.

A bulge in the insulation caught her attention as she turned. From any other angle it was virtually unnoticeable, but from that spot... Lucky find. She put her gloves back on and pulled the pink insulation away, mindful of the fiberglass spines, and pulled out an ornate box with drawings carved on it. No, she amended, tracing her gloved fingers over the box, not drawings. Hieroglyphs. Something she could translate with enough time.

"Ma'am, the police have arrived at the gate," Freddie reported. "We need to leave."

She needed to leave the box. Detective Morrow needed the evidence. Her fingers clenched it tightly. "Gimme three minutes." She pulled a camera out of her bag and began photographing every angle. She was still there when the police pulled up outside.

CHAPTER FIFTEEN

Dear Maria,

Hypothetically speaking, if I needed bail money and a place to hide for a few years until the statute of limitations expired, I could stay at your place... Right?

Delilah
P.S. Can I borrow some cash?

"HOW COULD YOU DO this to me?" Detective Morrow demanded.

Delilah sat in the uncomfortable interrogation chair, resolutely silent. They'd found Travys, handcuffed her, and now the lunch hour was toiling past with nothing to show for a hungry morning.

"Damn it, Delilah. How many times have I looked the other way? How many times? All you needed to do was call us. That's what the police get paid for, you know that, right? You know I earn my bread and butter chasing down criminals? While you earn your paycheck installing security cameras. Which is not what you did last night."

She closed her eyes, ready to relent, when there was a knock at the door.

"Hello?"

Delilah twisted in her seat, wide-eyed and furious.

The man in the doorway wore a tailored three-piece Dior suit. There was a touch of silver at his temples, and a charmingly smug smile on his face. "Detective Morrow?" Her father held out his hand. "I'm Miss Samson's legal counsel."

Morrow crossed his arms. "Really? Here I thought she'd done nothing more than tamper with evidence and interfere with the scene of a crime."

"She didn't do that," Doctor Charm said with easy reassurance.

Morrow's bulldog face wrinkled in confusion, but he started nodding.

"Miss Samson went to rescue her intern only moments before the police. She has no ulterior motive."

"No ulterior motive," Morrow murmured. He shook his head, trying to shake the effects of Daddy's Agree-With-Me-Ray. Since it had never worked on Delilah, she couldn't say she sympathized, but it had a similar effect on the boys she'd used it on in high school. Daddy had read her the riot act after that little stunt.

"If you bring us the evidence, we can sort everything out and be on our way. Miss Samson doesn't need to stay here any longer."

"Evidence. I'll go get that." Morrow walked to the door nodding like a concussed chicken.

The handcuffs dropped to Delilah's lap with a metallic clink. "Daddy, I think you're over doing it," she said as he sat on the table.

He looked down at her with dark eyes that struck fear into law enforcement everywhere—the untouchable villain, the one who always got away. "What in the Sam Hill do you think you're doing?" The Texas twang was faked, but it made her giggle. "I drove by that nut house on the way through town. What are you mixed up in?"

"Nothing. Travys left his dorm at a weird hour so I followed. I've no clue what was going on, but if you can get my phone back I have pictures."

"This isn't about the Golden Hunt, is it? Your mother will have bovine-producing fits if you're nosing around them again. We've only just managed to get the FBI to stop calling, asking for your phone number."

"Was it Jake?"

"It was Jake."

She winced. "I'm so sorry. I really did not mean for him to get so attached. All I did was collaborate on the arrest. We never even had a meal together."

"Smith women are very easy to obsess over," her father said sympathetically. "Look at me, I met your mother once and couldn't stop thinking about her."

Delilah rolled her eyes. "I know. I've only heard the story a few thousand times."

"And one of these days you'll have a very similar story to tell. Some gentleman who captured your attention, or you, depending on the scenario." He stood up and straightened his tie. "Put the handcuffs back on, the detective is headed this way."

"Talk fast and don't melt his brains. Or ruin his career! Detective Morrow is a good resource and I like him."

Her father raised an inquisitive eyebrow.

"Not like that. He's a friend."

"Who you shared no information with and who doesn't consider you a friend. My darling daughter, you are getting a dictionary for Christmas." But he did touch the watch with his Agree-With-Me ray in it, so at least he was going to dial down the mind-to-Slurpy rays.

Detective Morrow came in with a large box. "Phone, bag, and this box you were holding when we arrived."

"I'd only just found it," Delilah said. "I found Travys tied up in the basement. While I waited for the ambulance, I walked around the house searching for other victims."

"What ambulance?" Morrow demanded. "The one you didn't call because you didn't report anyone missing and didn't call 911?" He slammed the box on the interrogation table. "I repeat, what the hell, Delilah?"

She crossed her arms.

"I think you might be a little out of your league," Doctor Charm said. "Do you have evidence gloves, detective? This isn't something I'd touch lightly."

"You recognize it?" Morrow asked.

Delilah frowned at the box in confusion. Hieroglyphs and languages were not Daddy's department.

"A number of years ago, when I was fresh out of law school, there was a bizarre kidnapping case in Colorado."

"The lotus blossom smell!" Delilah burst out.

"Precisely. I wouldn't be surprised to learn this once belonged to Lady Grimoire, matriarch of a significant branch of the superhero family tree back in the day. That was before The Company started pruning things to the point of extinction. An odd policy, I always thought. Very anti-superhero."

"Ahem." Delilah cleared her throat and kicked her father in the shin. "Back to the task at hand. Can I be re-leased? I'm starving, and tired, and I'm very late for work."

With a grave smile her father turned to the detective. "Naturally. Detective Morrow, I think you will need the expertise offered by Miss Samson. This is not an ordinary case."

"I need to know what happened," Morrow said.

"Miss Samson will write a statement, you will release her. I will liaise between the two of you until the killer is brought to justice."

"Killer?" Morrow looked at her. "What killer? I thought this was about your intern getting kidnapped."

"Travys was helping me review the mayor's case." Delilah shrugged. "He must have found more than he let on. Maybe he thought he could solve the case by himself. Too many movies about teenage spies and investigators I suppose. How is he doing? You've purposefully failed to mention his health this entire time."

Morrow grimaced in response. "He's fine. They gave him a pint of blood at the hospital, but otherwise he's fine. No drugs in his system, nothing that some bed rest and a few steaks won't fix."

"Tell me," her father said, "is blood theft a common crime in this area?"

"No." Morrow shook his head. "I've been on the force for over thirty years and I've seen some weird sh—stuff." He shuffled his feet a little at the slip up. "But this is new."

"An overly aggressive blood bank, perhaps?"

"Maybe." Morrow sighed. "All right, Delilah, I'll bring you the forms. Once the statement is filled out, I'll let you go. But that better be the most thorough document you've ever written. The chief is ready to eat me alive. You're our best contract worker and you screwed with a crime scene. Rookies aren't even that dumb and they can barely tie their own shoes."

* * *

Delilah walked out of the precinct two hours later in a huff. Half the day wasted and she was still hungry. Lunch, or an early dinner, that was the first course of action. Then she'd book Daddy Dearest a hotel, or a flight home, and check on Travys.

Then maybe she'd have time to search for a new job in the Help Wanted section before bed. It didn't matter what Wil said over the phone, she was sunk in Chicago. All that time carefully building a relationship with the police, growing her contacts list, making a place for herself... Gone. Straight down the loo. All because she trusted a handsome man not to abandon her.

Well, Alan Adale could keep his cold bed and shadowy hands to himself.

Superheroes and villains... Maybe it only worked if the girl was the good one. Her mom had been a superhero before marrying Doctor Charm, but her mother also had the kind of body that made men trip over themselves to please her. The best compliment Delilah had ever been offered was that she was regal. Most people called her stern. Or aloof. Or cold.

Cold seemed to be a favorite. Or the old stand-by: heartless.

Well, she tugged her gloves on and bit her lip, it happened. There were only so many times a girl could hear her date confess he asked her out for sex alone, or because he wanted to date her sister, but Angela was hard to talk to. Angela looked like Mom, and was sweet as honey and happily married, and—Delilah reminded herself firmly—it wasn't her sister's fault all males were born with only two brain cells and a couple ball sack's worth of stupidity. A het woman just had to roll with their infantile fascination with balls and accept the inevitable social gaffes.

Being a lesbian was growing more attractive by the hour.

"Delilah!" Alan's voice made her turn. "Are you crying? What's wrong? What's going on?"

She wiped her eyes and threw her head up. "I had something in my eye. What are you doing here?"

"I came to talk to Detective Morrow because I heard you were arrested."

"Yes, I was pulled in at four this morning. About five minutes after you left, actually. Convenient timing. But everything's fine now." She gave him a bright smile and tried not to think of stabbing him. Her New Year's resolution was going to be to date every blond man in the city. One by one she'd pick off the herd and break their hearts. It would be a cathartic exercise to complete before her passport arrived.

Hmmm. Passport.

She changed directions and headed for the nearest post office. An official passport would make life so much easier. Muddle the trail a bit. And she could switch names; Cassandra More, Ellie Fine, maybe Ann. Ann the librarian.

No, not a librarian. The temptation to get a job in New York would be too strong. She needed something that kept her out of the country a lot.

Alan caught up with her. "Where are you going?"

"Why do you care?" She stopped and glared at him. "Oh wait. You don't. Funny thing that."

"I do too and you know it."

She waited for the brutal cold that came with hard lies. Nothing happened.

"I got back to my office at ten, dealt with a ton of... Never mind. I'm sorry I didn't come back for you right away. The tunnel went all the way down town and I wanted to keep Kalydon in my sights. He and the Hunt went to somewhere off Lake Street. It's a mess. I need—"

"You aren't lying," Delilah said, interrupting.

Alan stared at her in confusion. "Why would I lie?"

"Because everyone tries to lie to me."

"I haven't."

Her heart raced as she tried to remember all their many conversations. Alan had never lied. There were implications there she wasn't quite ready to explore.

"Delilah?" Alan stepped forward.

And she stepped back.

"Hi, sweetheart." A heavy hand landed on Delilah's shoulder. "Am I interrupting anything?"

She looked up at her father. Replacing Alan would be as easy as finding another green-eyed blond with the body of Adonis and a dry sense of humor Terry Pratchett would envy. Replacing Daddy was infinitely more difficult. "Aren't you supposed to be somewhere? Catching a flight? Talking to Detective Morrow? Anything at all?"

"Nope. I was going to go buy you lunch and talk to you about all this. But it seems I'm going to make an awkward third wheel. Who is the nice young man?"

"Someone who is neither nice nor young," Delilah muttered, shooting Alan a glare that would have turned a lesser man to ash.

Alan frowned. "Delilah..."

"He knows your name?" Doctor Charm asked, reaching for his watch.

Delilah grabbed his hand to stop him. "Doctor Smith is a recent expert in strange languages like the one found on the box at the crime scene."

"What box?" Alan asked.

She ignored him. "Alderman Adale is Chicago's deputy mayor, the pro tem mayor under the circumstances. He's following the whole case very closely." The muscles in her shoulders tightened until she thought bone might break. "Don't you both have jobs? It's the middle of a work day!"

Alan raised an eyebrow. "Smith?"

"Yes."

"Then I assume I have the immeasurable pleasure of addressing the one and only Doctor Charm." Alan nodded his head in a semi-bow.

It was a terrible twist of fate that gave her the ability to unlock things but not break the earth apart to swallow her whole when she most needed it.

Daddy's eyebrow went up as he turned to her. "Where do you dispose of bodies in this town, sweetheart?"

"You can't kill him." She floundered for a second. "I don't have a reason why you can't kill him, but you can't. Dad, you need to go home. Right now. Leave town. Alan, you need to go to work. And erase my phone number. I'm going to lunch."

They both started following her.

She spun and faced them. "Alone! I am going to lunch alone." To think.

She stopped at the first hole-in-the-wall Mexican place she found and ordered the house special. After a glass of horchata and more guacamole than she strictly needed, the locks on the cupboards stopped popping open.

This needed to end. Tonight.

Alan said he'd chased Kalydon down the tunnels to the lake. There was a lot of ground to cover there. Plenty of places to enter the old bootlegging tunnels. The property on Wacker Street probably had a subterranean entrance, something the owner paid to keep off the public records.

Tonight, she'd find it and make them pay.

CHAPTER SIXTEEN

Dear Mom,

Can you remember to pack an extra stocking for Christmas? We might have a surprise visitor and I want to make sure there's enough to go around.

Love,
Delilah

WHITE WINE SWIRLED AROUND the inside of a crystal glass. Alinea had been known for its avant garde menu for nearly two decades, and the debonair Doctor Charm had danced past the maître d' as if there wasn't a two-week waiting list.

"Do you drink?" the doctor asked.

"No."

He put his glass aside. "So you are a superhero. It seems alcohol and mutations don't mix."

"Maybe I'm Mormon."

The doctor smirked. "I doubt it. I've met a few, and there's nothing in your background to suggest religious affiliation."

"You checked?" Alan asked, only mildly surprised.

"Wouldn't you check on the potential bachelors in a town your favorite child was moving to? There's a very short list of acceptable men out here."

Alan pretended to be interested in the menu. "Having children isn't a problem I have."

"Oh, do you have children already?"

He stopped reading, eyes widening in horror. "I meant I don't have any children to worry about!" Alan folded the menu in exasperation. "Why are we here?"

"I'm trying to help you," Doctor Charm said.

"How?"

The waiter stopped to refill Alan's water glass. "Are you ready to order, sir?"

"The Winter Sampler for two, please," Doctor Charm said. He paused while the waiter walked away before saying, "We have two options. One, I erase your memories of recent events. You won't remember your time with Delilah, but you won't have the heartache either."

Alan sipped his water. "Difficult to do, erasing nearly eighteen months of memory. The gaps would be noticeable."

"You haven't been close to Delilah that long."

"Not that you know of."

"My daughter keeps me apprised of what's happening in her life."

"Somehow I doubt she's always truthful. Delilah likes her secrets."

The doctor pursed his lips as the waiters delivered a terrarium of salad greens, accented with mushrooms houses and some unidentifiable food shaped into a red gnome hat. Frowning, he poked at the greens. "We should have flown to Paris. They know how to make a decent lunch there."

"But the customs wait would be too long," Alan quipped.

"Indeed, although there are numerous ways around that." He sighed and set his fork aside. "You seem like a very nice young man. But you don't realize how much trouble a woman can get you into. You think it will be all flowers, and cupcakes, and sex, and the next thing you know you're changing the oil in cars and rocking colicky babies to sleep at three in the morning. Liking her long legs isn't enough to build a relationship on."

"You think the only reason I care about Delilah is how attractive she is?"

Doctor Charm shrugged. "You wouldn't be the first."

"I'm not like those men."

"In that case, you're going to need a better arsenal. Tell me, do you have a bulletproof vest?"

* * *

Raw earth, cement, old brickwork... Delilah ran her hand along the tunnel wall deep under Chicago proper. It was like a dark fantasyland. The ghost of jazz music flitted through her mind, a memory of a simpler time.

Or perhaps not. Perhaps superheroes were only the next evolution to it all. Kalydon was the new Al Capone, the shady business baron dealing magic elixirs in the dark. And she was Elliot Ness, the untouchable, incorruptible dealer of justice.

The thought made her grin in the darkness as her flashlight panned ahead of her, looking for security cameras and doors into the Wacker building overhead. Something rat-sized moved in the shadows ahead, shuffling and digging, but not moving away. It twitched, then fell still as she walked closer. The toe of a heavy work boot pointed upward, the edge of a leg of denim pants barely visible through a layer of heavy mud.

For a moment her mind couldn't quite grasp what she was seeing. And then it all clicked. Someone was buried alive under the muddy floor. Or, at least, they had been alive when she'd started walking toward them.

Stretching her hand over the packed dirt, she tried to loosen everything. But the dirt wasn't locked per se, it was just there, and she hadn't thought to bring a shovel for breaking and entering.

A hand clawed through the mud. Delilah grabbed it, pulling the hapless victim out of the grave. The mud-covered face was barely recognizable as Ivan with a broken nose. "You?"

"Me." Delilah squatted down and looked him in the eye. "What happened?"

"They decided I was expendable."

Focusing on Ivan, Delilah loosened her grip on her talent. His pupils dilated even wider than before. He stared at her with a glazed expression.

"Tell me everything," she said.

"The Mégisti formula gives normal people superpowers. Flight. Strength. Health. The seller proved it to us. Shot one of his men, gave him the formula and healed him in front of us. Said he needed money and a volunteer."

"And you got volun-told?" Delilah guessed.

"Seller said I was wrong. His guy punched me. It was like being hit by a car. I woke up choking on dirt." He paused, reaching for his still buried legs. "I think I broke a bone."

Delilah blew a stray hair out of her eye. "Where's the entrance?"

"Don't know. Wasn't conscious when they brought me in." Ivan rocked back as his eyes returned to normal. "I hurt."

"Can you wait twenty minutes, or should I call the police?"

He stared out into the darkness. "Got an extra flashlight?"

She took her phone out, turned on the GPS, and put a lock on it. "Here."

Ivan turned it over in his muddy hand and grinned. "You're going to leave your phone here for me to hack?"

"Yeah, that's exactly it." Delilah rolled her eyes. "You unlock that and I'll buy you dinner." The Pentagon couldn't unlock her phone and she'd sold the prototype for the lock to them when she was in college. Good educations weren't cheap. When people asked about her sudden surge of wealth, she told them a rich uncle had left her money in his will.

It made you despair, it really did. Her entire life's history had been available if anyone had wanted to look, but they never had. Not a single person had considered her worth a full background check. Yet they'd given her the keys to every room on campus because she did work-study as an early morning janitor. The minions had done the cleaning, but still, they'd handed over the keys! Humanity.

Walking along the broken wall, intensely aware of Ivan watching her, she wondered why she thought the keys had mattered anyway. Doors were just bigger keyholes.

A flutter of warm air caressed her hand through the chipped mortar. Somewhere on the other side was a heat source. She focused, and the wall crumpled to dust under her fingers. With a quick smile at Ivan, she stepped through the hole and into a section of the Chicago pedway illuminated only by emergency lighting.

Odd, for this time of day. The pedway closed at five but there were usually lights on down here, homeless people, and all the other little joys of subterranean Chicago life. She sniffed the air, inhaling dust and bleach.

Taking the handheld GPS out of her pocket, she pinged the satellite quickly and confirmed her suspicions; she was under 77 Wacker Drive. Someone had boarded up this area to use as a private entrance to the mostly-abandoned building.

Turning the GPS off so it didn't attract unwanted electronic attention, she found the signs for the exit and followed the concrete stairs upwards. Three flights up the stairs changed, wooden doors dividing the bare concrete from padded floors covered in a rich tapestry carpet with maroon and gold accents.

There was a lock on the door. Relying on the tech gad-gets she'd borrowed from her father to handle any unseen security, she swept past it.

The hall didn't feel lived in. It smelled like a mausoleum, all death and dust and forgotten dreams. Maybe in some ways it was. If Kalydon was behind this—and she had no reason to believe he wasn't—then he was running out of time. Money couldn't buy him immortality. She wasn't even sure why someone would want to buy immortality. Death wasn't frightening. It was simply there—like the night sky, or the ocean, or a mountain.

An old man bent and broken by the indelicacies of age should embrace death. It was a release of pain, a final farewell to every sorrow. But maybe that was only a young person's point of view. Perhaps, after a few more decades, life would become such a terrible addiction that she too would view death with fear.

If she died today her mother's fury would bring her back to life long enough for a harangue that never ended.

Two more flights of stairs and Delilah found herself looking at a row of basic conference rooms with windows in the doors and a few computers— old boxy machines that were new when her parents married, but computers nonetheless. At the very end of the corridor was a different door, white with the black number nine hanging in the center, like one would find hanging on the front of house in any urbanized area. Like Atlanta, to pick a not-so-totally-random example.

Delilah quirked her lips in a smile, tugged her black leather gloves on, and opened the door.

She waited for a minute, watching the interior gloom to see if anything moved. No sirens screamed. No lights flashed a warning. Everything was deadly quiet.

Stepping inside as she closed the door behind her, she flicked on her flashlight. The carpet continued here and pictures hung on the wall, none of them spectacular. Hunting prints for the most part. Cheap posters of green tractors, bird hunters, and deer standing under autumn leaves, all in expensive frames. Dusty bookcases with leather-bound books, covers dirty and cracking from age, lined the wall.

A deer head hung on one wall next to an over-stuffed red chair. In another corner she saw a stuffed grizzly bear. Kalydon liked trophies, but she suspected those were from his younger days. The rooms flowed together to another set of stairs, another lock she snapped open, and another set of lavishly appointed rooms in the same dark red plush and velvet.

There was an air of opulence here, but not of cultivated taste. It was as if Kalydon had seen a picture of a wealthy home and bought everything out of a catalog. Or maybe she was biased because red velvet was so very 1970-something.

It was an interior apartment with no obvious windows, but even in bright sunshine this room would be gloomy. The furniture was all heavy wood stained black. The fabric on the rugs and the curtains framing a black-and-white image of the New York skyline pre-9/11 were all deep red, almost crimson. Bookcases covered a wall in here too, but a cursory glance told her these weren't normal books. These were in shades of sand and earth, mixed with an eclectic choice of statuary. The bust of a woman carved out of a black stone with a gold skull erupting from her face was the focal point.

Delilah leaned forward and sniffed at the books. Without a lab it was impossible to tell, but they looked suspiciously like examples she'd seen of auto-anthropodermic bibliopegy from the seventeenth century: books bound in human skin. The grotesque practice had fallen out of favor fairly quickly, but these didn't appear to be all that ancient.

Shivers of apprehension crawled up her back like an icy spider walking on her spine.

There was another door, this one with a combination lock, and for most lock picks it would have presented an interesting diversion for several hours. Delilah opened it with a glance and stepped into the room she'd been dreading, but knew all along she would find. It was no bigger than a jail cell on death row, ten feet by ten feet perhaps. There was one chair, a match to the one down-stairs, a fake fireplace that was turned off, and a rug of pale leather. Bare skin...

Human, unless she missed her guess completely, al-though the hair and fingers rather gave it away.

Revulsion and bile filled her mouth. She wondered which of the faces on the wall once belonged to the rug. She recognized several of them. The Wooden Wonder and Mayor Arámbula were on one wall with clippings from the newspaper taped next to their pictures. On another wall she saw street photos, men and women Kalydon had stalked perhaps... But no. Up at the top was a row of smiling faces.

The Hunt.

The Golden Hunt of Atlanta was pictured with their victims tallied below them like some sick scavenger hunt. She pulled out her micro-camera and started snapping pictures. As she zoomed in on a familiar face, something else tore her attention downward.

Travys's mother. Thinner than when she'd left New York. Haggard. But unmistakably Travys's mother, walking through the Peachtree Plaza in Atlanta. Up above was the late mayor's toady, Chasten Huntley. Even his name fit.

She took a few more pictures and then stepped out, fusing the door shut behind her by unlocking all the molecules and letting them melt together. Kalydon didn't seem like the sort of man who understood subtle gestures. That was fine. What she had in mind was about as subtle as a jackhammer.

There was only one last place she wanted to search: Kalydon's bedroom. People of his ilk kept what they loved close. The kill room was a toy room, really. Some people had places to watch TV, and sociopaths kept rooms full of tokens stolen off their victims. It probably balanced out in the scheme of things. But Kalydon had been raised in the Deep South and in deep poverty, which meant money in the mattress and a gun safe in the bedroom.

After several false starts she found the bedroom. It wasn't hard to see how deep Kalydon's roots were. Under the expensive coverlet was a set of plaid flannel sheets. It seemed like a waste. All that wealth and ambition wrapped up in the brains of a chicken. She pulled a hunting print to the side and glared at the gun safe. It swung open, revealing an array of guns that would keep a small dictatorship in power for at least a year, and a row of test tubes with a glowing blue liquid. Bingo.

Delilah scooped the test tubes up, wrapped them in a pillowcase stripped from the bed, and put them in her bag. Now, how to let Kalydon know what she wanted? Maybe something written in red...

CHAPTER SEVENTEEN

Noah,

You better get your butt back safe and sound or you will never hear the end of it. If you make my baby sister cry I will move Heaven, Earth, and Hell to make sure you pay. There is nowhere on this planet or in near orbit that you can hide from me. And you know you can't fight me because your mother will ground you if you hit a girl. She won't care how old you are. So keep that in mind. Merry Christmas.

Come home safe,
Delilah

A SURLY IVAN WAITED for her in the depths of Chicago's tunnels. "About bloody time you got back. I thought you were gone for good."

"I ran out of lipstick and had to go buy more."

His face contorted into a horrified grimace. "What would happen to me if you died?"

"You'd be motivated to unlock my phone," Delilah said as she squatted beside him. "Figure out the code yet?"

"Hmph." He rolled his eyes and held the muddy phone out. "It's not a phone, is it?"

"It's a phone, but it's my phone, which is why it's customized."

"Voids the warranty if you do that," Ivan muttered.

She scraped the mud aside so he could see the insignia. "This look like a brand you know? I doubt it."

"You make your own phones? Don't you have any life at all?"

"I don't make my phones. I own stock in a small company that makes custom phones for wealthy professionals."

Another eye roll.

"How are you feeling?"

"Both legs broken, maybe a rib. You going to drag me out of here or call the police to come pick me up?" He was the very picture of stoic despair, the beaten villain brought low.

Delilah smirked, an expression he doubtless didn't see in the darkness. "That all depends." She pulled one of the vials out of her bag. "Do you know what this is?"

"The Mégisti formula, Greek for great or something like that." Ivan shrugged. "My boss wants it.

Seller had it. But the deal went south." He paused and frowned. "How'd you get it?"

"I took it out of the wall safe."

"Out of..." Ivan spluttered in frustration. "Do you know what I've done to get my hands on that in the past two weeks? I've tied myself in knots! Begged. Bribed. Threatened. Cut throats." He switched to Russian for a good long tirade. "Bloody woman! How'd you get the safe combination? Tell me!"

Delilah raised an eyebrow. "Combination? Why would I do that when the doors all unlocked for me?"

Even in the darkness she could see him flushing red with rage.

She held the formula out. "What happens if you ingest this?"

"According to the seller?"

She nodded.

"It's a magic potion that heals you, gives you super strength, superhuman speed, flight. There was something about distilling proteins from blood of freaks and finding the right balance of whatever. I don't know." Ivan shrugged. "Sounds like a lot of nonsense to me."

"Did Kalydon try to use this on you?"

Ivan's brow wrinkled in confusion. "Is that the seller's name? I didn't know." But now he did and there was more than a hint of retribution in his tone. "He didn't offer it to me. He wanted blood."

"And not as in revenge?"

"Nah, two of his thugs grabbed me as soon as my boss dropped me off. Popped a needle into my vein like I'm some damn junkie." His shoulders hunched over at the memory. "But something went wrong. I wasn't right." He shook his head.

Delilah shook the vial. "Drink up."

Ivan scowled at her.

"It might heal you. It might kill you. But I'm leaving now, and this is your one chance to get out of here."

"What? You're leaving me? I thought we were friends! We had this whole villainous rapport with each other. Witty banter was exchanged."

She laughed. "You really are delusional. Drink up. If you survive, you can rescue yourself."

"And if I don't?"

She shrugged. "I'm sure someone will find you. Eventually."

* * *

"Rescue me!" Travys shouted as soon as Delilah entered the room. "You have to get me out of here. There's nothing on TV but shows about house hunting and bread baking."

Delilah's four-inch heels clicked on the hospital room linoleum. "Those are useful life skills."

"I'm going to die of boredom. Also, I'm going to die if I miss my finals and can't play basketball because my grades are too low."

"You'll also die if the Golden Hunt of Atlanta finds you," Delilah said. "Which is why you're leaving the city."

Travys's jaw dropped.

"Your doctor is signing the release forms as we speak, and your luggage is packed."

"You can't do that to me!"

She lifted her chin with a small smile. "You'll find there's very little in life that I can't do."

"Delilah, you can't," Travys said. "I'm so close to finding my mom. I know the answer's here. That guy knows."

"Yes. And now the police know." She let that sink in. "It's over. All that's left is the wrap up."

He narrowed his eyes. "If it's over, why do I need to go anywhere? I'm safe."

"This isn't a police show on the television. Sometimes wrap-up takes more than five minutes. People run. People fight. You have already been injured and I won't let that happen a second time."

He slammed his head back into the pillows, making the hospital bed quake. "She's dead, isn't she?"

"Yes."

He stared at the wall. "Why don't I feel anything?"

Delilah sat on the edge of his bed. "You've suspected this for a long time. Maybe you've already done your grieving. Or maybe it will come later. Or maybe you never will. Sometimes, when we can't handle an emotion, it's like a phantom limb. You feel the pain and it never goes away."

"I knew she was dead last year." He turned away to look out the window. "The guy who did it?"

"Dead."

"Good." Travys nodded and turned back to her. "So which relative are you foisting me off on? My aunt? My cousins? Maybe Chris is out of jail and we could have some dick-son bonding time over the holidays."

"Don't be ridiculous. You're going to California to stay with Angela, Ty, and Aaron."

Travys gave her some serious side eye. "For real?"

Angela, as always, had perfect timing. She walked in, wearing flip-flops totally unsuitable for the snowstorm outside. "Hey! How's my favorite student!"

Travys chuckled weakly. "Hi, Miss Smith. I'm good. I'm doing real well on my math..." He turned as pale as a boy with ancestors from Zambia could get. "Son of... My math final is tomorrow! Miss Smith, ya gotta let me stay! My final is tomorrow!"

Angela smiled and smoothed his hair back. "Handled. I went and talked to the dean about everything today, then spoke with your teachers. They're going to let me proctor the test at home. You can take it as soon as we get to the house if you want."

Travys grimaced. "That's going to be what, three in the morning? No offense, Miss Smith, but I'm not ready for a test after a plane ride."

Delilah covered a smirk with her hand as Angela stared at Travys in utter confusion. "Arktos doesn't need a plane," she said softly. "But I do need to get going. It's after eight and I've had a long day."

Tyler Running-Fox, once the most eligible bachelor in America and still considered by most to be the handsomest man in the world, stepped into the room with a bevy of nurses floating in his wake.

"Oh, joy, you brought gawkers." Delilah frowned.

Ty shrugged. "I had to show them my ID to get in. What did you want me to do?"

"Lie," Delilah said. "Remind me to make you a fake ID sometime. How do you feel about being Carlos Manoso?"

"Leave my favorite books out of this," Ty said, pointing a warning finger at her. "I am man enough to admit I like funny books."

Angela and Delilah shared an exasperated sister look. No one else could possibly understand the pain of their mother's obsession with a clumsy bounty hunter from New Jersey who churned through cars faster than Daddy did through first-generation minions. Some people went door-to-door selling religion; Mom was a zealot bent on sharing the wonders of nineties romance novels cum noir detective tales.

"I hold you fully responsible," Angela said. "If you hadn't left them alone while I was getting changed to go out for dinner, Mom never would have handed him the book."

Ty leaned over and kissed Angela's forehead. "It's just a book. Let's get the kiddo out of here. We still have a party to go grocery shopping for."

"Party?" Travys perked up. "I like parties!"

"Aaron's having an end-of-semester bash with some of his school friends," Angela said with a slinky cat-that-ate-the-canary grin. Oh, yeah, Delilah's big sis knew the way to make men do what she wanted. "Ever heard of DJ South?"

"The singer?" Travys's voice hit a high note in excitement.

"That's her. She lives next door, so Aaron invited her to drop by for the pool party tomorrow. She's already confirmed she'll be there."

Travys held out his arm with the blood pressure monitor. "I'm ready to go."

CHAPTER EIGHTEEN

Alan,

The Hunt has captured Travys again. I don't know how they got him out of the hospital, but they did. I'll call as soon as I know anything.

Love,
Delilah

DELILAH PULLED HER KEVLAR under-armor on and strapped a knife to her leg. It was on the small side, but it was all for show anyway.

"I don't like this," Freddie muttered.

"It doesn't matter," she said as she pulled her black dress on. She turned in front of the mirror, watching to see how the skirt fell. Perfect.

Freddie handed her a red wool coat with silk lining. "You should have asked for backup, not sent the one ally you have on a wild goose chase."

"And how would Alan help, exactly? He can't do anything to hurt the Golden Hunt. He can't risk exposing who he really is. It would be political suicide at best. Telling him Travys was kidnapped again keeps him safe." Worse, the Hunt was waiting for the Spirit of Chicago. In her gut she knew they were hunting him. But he was hers now, and they could have him when they pried him from her cold, dead hands. Sending him on a wild goose chase to the south of town had been the best she could do, but it should keep him safe long enough for her to deal with the mess.

"Why aren't we calling the police and getting a SWAT team in there?" Freddie asked.

"One, because at least one of Kalydon's minions has taken the Mégisti formula and has super speed, so any normal human would be killed, and two, because they hurt Travys. He's one of the family, and people who hurt the family don't walk away from me."

Freddie snorted.

"I watched Ivan after he took a drink," Delilah continued. "Two broken legs working in minutes, and he moved faster than any human could. Even Mom doesn't fly that fast. The only way I can take the Hunt down is if I get them to sit still, and you get more flies with honey than vinegar. Kalydon fancies himself a made man, attractive and wonderful. He wants me now."

"Because you vandalized his apartment."

She waved a dismissive hand. "It was a note written on his mirror."

"And who is to watch to see that no one else interferes with this take down?" Freddie asked. "The Russians haven't abandoned their course. The Company might still be in town."

"I'm counting on it." The Company had hurt her family too, but that was the beauty of her plan. If everything went according to her script, she'd be able to pay The Company back tenfold. "Let's go."

The drive over was silent. Freddie kept giving her hurt looks in the mirror.

"Go home," Delilah ordered as she stepped out of the cab. "I'll be back within seventy-two hours."

"And if you aren't?" the minion demanded.

"Then, and only then, may you call in the cavalry." She slammed the door shut. Anticipation warmed her like nothing else could. Too long the Golden Hunt had prowled her city, hunted her people, hurt the ones she loved. And now it was time for a reckoning.

* * *

Alan's phone screamed with a ringtone he hadn't programmed in as he steered the car smoothly through the traffic. He hit the call button on the dash. "Delilah?"

"No."

It took him a moment to place the gravelly voice on the other end of the line. "Freddie?" he asked in disbelief.

"Yes, sir." There was a silence. A very obedient silence, as if Freddie was trying to fill it with all the things he wasn't supposed to say.

"Where's Delilah?" he said, dreading the answer.

"I'm so glad you asked, sir," Freddie replied. "She's gone for a drive up town to meet a certain huntsman I've been specifically forbidden to talk about. While I can't name the bastard, I can say that my mistress is visiting him at his Chicago domicile and nowhere south of Lake Michigan near the address she sent you."

"How circuitous," Alan said as something to say while his brain raced. Delilah was going to meet Kalydon. Alone. In Chicago. And she'd sent him out of the city on purpose. "Where is Travys?"

"I have been specifically forbidden to mention the young gentleman's whereabouts, or the fact that a certain family member stopped by late last evening to collect the young gentleman's coat that he had left here inadvertently."

Alan snorted. "I like how that forbidden bit keeps you from saying anything. Very effective."

"I was programmed for loyalty, sir, not stupidity," Freddie said primly.

"Delilah is going to have your ears when she realizes what you've done." Alan took the highway exit and stopped at a light so he could get back on 90 North.

Freddie was silent for a moment. "Miss Delilah may very well be upset, but within the parameters of my pro-gramming and understanding, I'm not sure. She may have anticipated this phone call. It's the only reason I could call."

"She forbade you to call but you think she expected you to call me anyway?" The light turned green and he drove under the overpass.

"There's a twenty-three percent chance that my mistress anticipated this phone call and your return at the right moment."

Alan's gripped tightened on the wheel. "Wouldn't it have been easier for Delilah to tell me when she wanted me to show up and save the day?"

"I couldn't say, sir. The mistress's mind is a mystery to me."

"Me too." Alan sighed. "I'll be there in about forty minutes if the traffic stays steady."

"Sir, if I could be so forward, I would recommend breaking a few of the more pedestrian traffic laws. Miss Delilah entered the building over ten minutes ago, and I didn't call until the building sealed itself. We're unable to reach her, sir." Worry underscored Freddie's words.

Alan's foot flattened the accelerator. "I'll be there in time." Even if he had to ditch the car and ghost his way to Chicago.

"Miss Samson, what a pleasant surprise." Kalydon's voice dripped with contempt as she stepped inside the shadowy room. He moved a wrinkled hand and she heard the door seal behind her with a smothered thump.

Delilah looked around the room, matching the faces visible in the gloom to the pictures on Kalydon's Kill Wall. "My, my, my, the whole gang is here." She smiled. "What? No chair for me?"

"You volunteered yourself," Kalydon reminded her. "Your blood for the city of Chicago."

"And names in exchange for the formula," Delilah said, stripping off her gloves. "Thankfully I'm young enough that senility and dementia haven't set in yet."

Klaydon growled at the insult.

Her smile grew sweeter.

"Blood first," said a woman's voice. She stepped out of the gloom, revealing obsidian black skin and a shimmering gold dress. Her hair was white and tied up in a hundred small braids. "Do you know me?"

"Ayo Naiabi," Delilah said. "I know your reputation. Child soldier in Africa, brought to England by an international charity group, suspected of your boyfriend's murder in college but you were found not guilty in court."

"Murder is between equals," Ayo said. "One such as myself can never murder a human, only exterminate them."

"Yet you cried on the stand and declared you loved him," Delilah mocked softly. "Such love, you said. Such devotion."

"Like a dog." Ayo shrugged. "He was my pet, and when he became unruly I put him down."

Kalydon thumped his cane on the ground. "Enough. The blood, Miss Samson. A donation to our work."

"To your longevity you mean? That is what you use this serum for isn't it, Kalydon? You keep the Grim Reaper at bay with these injections, but they're not working as well as before." She brushed past Ayo to sit down in the empty chair. "That's why the murders have become more frequent, isn't it?"

The old man glared at her. "Nonsense."

"Perfect sense," Delilah countered. "The formula first became available in 1985, a product of a villain called Lady Grimoire. She produced small amounts using her own blood as part of the Eden Project. Of course that was before she considered a villain, wasn't it? She was plain, ordinary Marjorie Thayer, single mother and biochemist, when she worked for Kalydon Industries."

"I don't know what you're talking about," Kalydon said stiffly.

"Liar." Delilah winked at him and relaxed. "Marji was one of your little failures, wasn't she? You mentioned her in an interview once. A brilliant scientist who spurned you because your wealth wasn't enough to blind her to your other failings."

"I have no failings!"

"Hubris being chief amongst your faults," Delilah continued as if he'd said nothing. "When The Company was formed and Project Eden was taken away from her, Marjorie quit. She left you, went rogue, became a villain. Her black market formula for superpowers created dozens of one-shot villains. Angry men and women who thought a single dose would make them gods. What's funny about people who want to become gods is that they're never happy with that first elevation, are they? No one with power is content. We all want more. I want stronger powers to be like the other superheroes." It was a plausible lie, especially to someone like Kalydon who lived with the More Is More mentality. "You wanted superpowers to prove Marjorie, and everyone else who mocked you, wrong. Ayo wants revenge. Chasten Huntley," she waved to the mayor's social secretary, "wants attention. I bet we could ask everyone here if they want more power and they'd all say yes."

Ayo shrugged. "So? We are the pinnacle of evolution. We are the wise ones. The brave ones. The warriors."

"No, warriors fight for a cause," Delilah said. "You're power-hungry fools."

Kalydon stood. Rage radiated off him like a perfume as he shook. "How dare you," he said between clenched teeth. "How dare you challenge me? I have laid low your protectors of humanity, your so-called heroes. I have hunted them like the animals they are!"

"And?" Delilah asked calmly.

"I am better than they are!"

"Because you pulled a trigger?"

"Yes!"

She clapped ironically. "Bravo! You are a tool-using monkey! What a smart monkey."

Something moved behind her, grabbed her arm and twisted it up. "Do you know me?" an angry voice asked.

Delilah scanned the room and picked the missing name from the list. "Winda Leverick? From Boston?"

"Yes." He pushed her arm to the point of breaking. "Guess what I took a dose of this morning?"

"Oh, hmm. Let me guess. Mégisti?"

"That's right. I can rip your arms from your body, run faster than a train, fly like a bird in the wind. Can you, little girl with a big mouth?"

Delilah laughed. "Do I need to? I'm exactly where I want to be."

"Gag her," Kalydon ordered. "Get the machine out here. I won't waste any more time with her talk."

Leverick held her wrist tight enough to bruise, but the Megisti formula had its flaws. That's why notes mattered. That's why old records about dead people were worth reading. The serum numbed the nerves of the skin; it was the only way for a normal person to move at high speeds without writhing in pain.

Someone born with super-powered flight or speed wasn't using muscle, they were using magnetics, a fact Delilah learned all about from her mother. But Lady Grimoire's potion numbed the pain receptors and pumped extra oxygen into the muscles to allow a person to move at inhuman speeds.

Which meant that Leverick didn't feel the heat rising in the room until it was too late.

Kalydon wiped sweat from his forehead. "What is that? Who turned on the heater?"

"I feel nothing," Ayo said.

"Are you feeling well, sir?" Chasten asked, moving at a speed he wasn't born to.

Delilah smiled as the floor under her sagged.

"You!" Kalydon shoved an angry finger in her face. "What are you doing?"

"Unlocking things," Delilah said with a laugh. "That's my talent, didn't you know? The ability to unlock things. I can open doors. Make people tell me their secrets. It's a small, worthless, unimportant talent. Not very grand. Not very showy."

Ayo screamed as the floor under her collapsed.

"What are you doing?" Kalydon demanded.

"Unlocking the bonds between atoms."

She wasn't sure Kalydon had time to register what she said. It was possible he didn't even know what she meant. But he saw the results. One controlled atom bomb going off in his secret bunker on Wacker Street. After that, he probably didn't see very much at all.

CHAPTER NINETEEN

Dear Mom.

No matter what you hear, don't worry about me. I'm fine.

I love you,
Delilah

BRIGHT LIGHTS SWAM IN Delilah's field of vision. First little sparks, then pale yellow, then a strobing red and blue. A fireman in yellow pulled a rock aside. "Are you alive, miss?"

"I'm fine." Bruised, possibly with a fractured ankle, but fine.

Police cars swarmed the scene. She almost wished she could call them off. There was nothing left to find. The Golden Hunt hadn't been bombed, they were the bomb. In time, hopefully, someone would find the bunker with the kill wall. She'd done her best to keep the heat away from the room, but explosions were such an imprecise science. At least, done her way they were an imprecise science. A gifted arsonist could probably have left the room wholly untouched.

In the muzzy-headed way of the lightly concussed, Delilah knew this was an unproductive line of thought. There were people. Soon there would be questions. It wouldn't hurt to have a doctor look at her ankle or her head. But all she wanted to do was lie in the rubble and take a nap. Curl up around the still-warm chunks of concrete and sleep for a good twelve hours. For the first time in over a year, she relaxed. Everyone was safe. The Hunt was gone.

The fireman was carrying her to a waiting ambulance. News reporters flocked around. It was all a lot of fuss for one little girl from Texas.

"Delilah?" Detective Morrow pushed an EMT aside to get to her. "What were you doing here?"

"Following a lead." She managed to keep the smug self-satisfaction out of her voice.

Morrow folded his arms across his chest. "You okay?"

"I'm not dead," Delilah said. "Just tired."

"Don't go to sleep!" Morrow said at the same time as one of the emergency responders.

An EMT stepped forward. "Could be a concussion."

"Maybe one of the falling rocks hit me," Delilah said.

Morrow frowned. "Were you in the build—"

"Stop!" An elderly woman in white high heels picked her way across the rubble, a black wallet with a badge in it in hand. "Homeland Security. This is my witness."

The EMT smiled genially. "Sure thing. Let me get her checked out and we'll turn her over to you."

Detective Morrow looked like a fish out of water. "Homeland Security? I thought you guys disbanded. We don't need you here. A building collapse doesn't make it federal jurisdiction."

"A terrorist bombing does," the woman said with a snide smile. "It was a bomb, wasn't it, Miss Smith?"

Old memories of a darker time invaded Delilah's peace. "Katrina?"

The woman's smile grew sharper.

"You need to update your files. The name's Samson, not Smith."

"Either way," Katrina said. "You're coming with me."

Delilah weighed her options. Morrow would stop this if she objected. The EMT could be dealt with, and he undoubtedly had something in his kit that would make her head stop aching. It was the sight of a green-eyed blond on the other side of the police cordon that stopped her from making a fuss. Alan.

Freddie must have called him in. Either that or he'd ghosted to the national park address she'd sent, found no Travys, and come back to Chicago to find her. Katrina was reaching for her handcuffs. Things were a hair's breadth away from escalating.

The handcuffs clinked together and it was all Delilah could do not to laugh. Across the wreckage, she sent Alan a very firm glare. Hopefully he'd do the smart thing and stay away.

Katrina didn't get the joke though. She cuffed Delilah's hands behind her back and pushed her towards a waiting car. Delilah snickered quietly. Things couldn't have gone better if she'd written this script herself.

* * *

"Would you like some water?" The woman asking Delilah wore a black leather catsuit with a red slash down the left side and used a tone of menace that turned a drink of water into the promise of death.

Not that Delilah was going to eat or drink anything The Company offered, but even if she hadn't known Lead Feather's affiliations, she would have given the woman wide berth. "I'm fine. Thanks for asking."

Lead Feather sneered at her. "It's going to be such a pleasure to wipe that smile off your face."

"I'm sure you'll enjoy trying." Delilah relaxed in the uncomfortable chair. Her head was better, although her ankle still twinged. Running was out of the question, but The Company wanted to talk and she wanted to get some answers. It was a win-win scenario at the moment. "Are you going to take these cuffs off?"

"You wish," Lead Feather said. "Enjoy your new brace-lets. They'll be a permanent feature in your life."

The interrogation room door swung open and Katrina, Company boss, stepped inside. "Lead Feather, what are you doing here?" she chided. "Get to cleaning up."

"Yes, ma'am." With one last death glare, Lead Feather stepped out of the room.

When Delilah's mother was a young superhero working for The Company under the name Zephyr Girl, Katrina had been a hard-nosed woman with power suits and a Margret Thatcher haircut. In the decades since Zephyr Girl had 'died,' very little about Katrina had changed. Her dark hair had gone steel gray, she'd lost weight, and wrinkles had appeared, but on the whole she was very much like the woman Delilah had grown up seeing pictures of.

If you ever see this woman, you come get Mommy or Daddy right away. Do you understand, Delilah? Don't talk to her. Don't follow her. Don't unlock things near her. Her name is Katrina, and she is dangerous.

Some children grew up with the bogeyman; the Smith children grew up knowing The Company was lurking in the dark to kidnap them. Facing her childhood nightmare now, Delilah wanted to laugh. A chicken-boned woman with a smile like a ruler wasn't scary. She was pathetic. Delilah grinned like a shark. "Katrina, I've heard so much about you. I'm so glad you could fit me into your busy schedule."

Katrina's eyes narrowed into dark gimlets of fury. "Where's the formula?"

"Which formula?"

"The one that makes superheroes. The one Kalydon was peddling and that you were trying to steal when the bomb went off. It's out there. Six vials were sold at auction yesterday, but Kalydon said he had more."

Delilah leaned as far forward as she could. "Did you buy those six vials?"

"No. We're negotiating for the purchase of the formula."

Delilah's gaze fell on the window of bullet-proof glass and the empty offices beyond. "So it's true. The Company is losing superheroes."

"Like a sieve," Katrina confirmed. "It's the only reason you're alive. Twenty years ago we had over three hundred superheroes in the Midwest alone. Now there's one."

"That's a pretty high rate of retirement."

With a wintry smile Katrina said, "Superheroes don't retire. They die."

"No more heroes. No more mutant babies. No more Company?" Delilah guessed. "Maybe you should convince the super villains to switch sides."

"We tried," Katrina said through gritted teeth. "There's fewer of them every day too."

Delilah shrugged. "Have you ever considered the fact that there are superheroes out there, they just aren't signing up to do their patriotic duty? Maybe they don't like Company policy."

"Nonsense." Katrina either didn't know what Delilah's talent was, or hadn't taken precautions against it. She rambled on. "My daughter was born a superhero. I've done everything to keep her safe. Do you see grandchildren?"

"Maybe you were playing it a little too safe. Can't have the grandbabies if she's using a condom."

Katrina's death glare put Lead Feather's to shame. "I'm going to bring you some paper. You will write a full confession. You will detail every skill you possess. I will read it. If I think for a minute you've left anything out, I'll bring my mind-raper in. You may not have met one before. The Company doesn't keep one on staff, but the Russians loaned us Boris as a show of goodwill. I'm sure you and he will get along like a house on fire."

"There'll be nothing left?" Delilah smiled.

"Quite." Katrina stepped out, leaving a manila file folder with Delilah's information next to a blank sheet of paper and a pen. It was good to find a kindred soul who appreciated dead-tree documentation. Such a shame Katrina was a hubris-riddled fool.

The minute the door swung shut the handcuffs dropped to the ground. Delilah scribbled the word GOODBYE on the paper, took her file folder, and collapsed a bit of tile floor. Dropping into a supply closet was sheer dumb luck, but Delilah wasn't one to question providence. The locked door swung open at her touch, and she sauntered into the winter sunlight a free woman.

CHAPTER TWENTY

Delilah,

It's been a week and I don't know where you are. I miss you. There isn't an hour that goes past that I don't want to call you. I don't know if you'll ever forgive me, but please, let me know you're safe. If you get this email... let me know.

All my love,
Alan

ALAN SHOVED ANOTHER PILE of paperwork to the side. If he kept up this pace he might be able to find an end to the mess before the New Year rolled around.

The door opened and shut. He kept reading, scribbling his signature over highlighted portions and flipping pages as if his life depended on it.

The person who'd entered finally cleared their throat. "Boss?" It was Jesse, the office manager hired to replace the late Chasten Huntley.

"Yes?" Alan turned away from his computer reluctantly.

Jesse raised an eyebrow. "You do realize it's Christmas Eve, don't you?"

"Yes."

"Are you trying to be Scrooge?"

Alan blinked in confusion. The reference seemed to have no meaning. A vague recollection of a Muppet movie floated past. "You want to go home?"

"Everyone wants to go home, boss. Except you, and you're wearing the suit you wore yesterday."

Alan looked down at his shirt. "I changed my tie."

Jesse sighed. "Is this about the girl from the news?"

Delilah. Thinking about her in handcuffs made him want to run. To rescue her or to run away, he wasn't sure which. The Company had hauled her off while the building was still smoking and he'd been useless. Absolutely, infuriatingly useless. "It's not about her," he lied. "I just like to work."

"So it has nothing to do with the flowers that got returned from her office, or all those phone calls where no one answered?"

"No."

Jesse squinted at him. "Yeah. How'd you make it as a politician? You can't lie."

Alan shrugged. "An honest politician in Chicago? People voted for me because I have novelty value. It's like being the only unicorn in the petting zoo. Everyone thinks I'm pretty."

"I've got bad news for you, handsome. Unicorn or not, no woman is going to give you the time of day when you act like this. Go home, shower, sleep, order some Chinese food tomorrow and watch reruns of Christmas specials until you feel like puking. But don't come back to the office until the third."

"The third?" Panic took over. "What am I supposed to do with that much free time?"

"Sleep?" Jesse suggested. "Go grocery shopping? Scrub your sink? I don't know, what do single people do when they have time off? Get a hobby. Take up crochet, or something." He crossed the room, snatched up Alan's pen, and pointed at the door. "Time to call it a night, boss."

"Are you allowed to order me out of the office?" Alan asked as Jesse fished his coat out of the small office closet.

"That's what you pay me for. It's right in the contract, subsection B12: Make sure the office environment is healthy, safe, and pleasant for everyone. That includes monitoring overtime hours and making sure people don't kill themselves for the greater good of the city."

"I like the city," Alan protested feebly.

"And the city likes you," Jesse reassured him in a calm voice usually reserved for small, frightened children. "But it's not worth dying for."

No, only losing the love of his life for.

He let Jesse usher him out. Everyone else had gone home, limp garlands from the party he'd missed hung on the walls, another sad reminder of all he'd given up. Because he was a superhero. Because he was a freak. Because... He stepped outside into the snowy street. Chicago at rush hour on a holiday was never empty, but it felt that way. It was already getting dark and the snow was piling up. Alan trudged through it, kicking the slush in front of him.

The lobby was empty. He rode the elevator up alone. The silence wrapped around him and he walked to his front door like a man approaching the gallows. For a brief, shining moment he'd almost had everything he wanted. There had been the promise of a real holiday in front of him. He let the dream image of Delilah sitting with him by a Christmas tree surface in his memory once more. It was so real that for one sparkling second, he could almost smell her perfume as he fumbled for his keys.

The door fell open.

Delilah stood by the console table wrapped in a heavy black coat, lit only by the lights from the city outside, her hair and makeup a flawless shield. "I wondered how late you were planning on working," she said without preamble.

His mouth dried out. "How..."

She raised a perfectly sculpted eyebrow, her face an emotionless ivory mask. "They had me in hand-cuffs, Alan. How do you think I got away?"

Handcuffs... "Oh."

The faintest hint of a smile tugged at the corners of her mouth. "I'm glad you had the sense not to come rushing in. For a moment, I worried you'd think I was helpless."

"I did. I just didn't know what to do."

Delilah shrugged it away. "No matter. The Company gave me the information I wanted, so it all worked out on that end. You were the last loose thread I needed to take care of." She tapped a white envelope on the console table. "Your Christmas card. Happy holidays." She made eye contact, cool and deliberate and dismissive, and then swept past his reaching hand as if he was the least of her worries.

He probably was.

Alan sat in the dark as the scent of her perfume faded into the chill air. Christmas alone. Again.

He leaned against the console table and took a deep, shuddering breath. It hurt. It hurt almost as much as the time when he was six and thought that one family might actually adopt him. They'd been so nice, so sweet, and so generous. There'd been a mountain of toys bought and wrapped—and then on Christmas Eve the department of child services took him away. His adoption hadn't gone through.

He'd waited for them to come back, but they never did. They'd found another adoption agency, another little boy, and his one chance for happiness was gone without a trace.

His hand clenched around the envelope, and he felt something hard. Quickly, Alan flipped on a lamp and ripped the envelope open. A Christmas card with a horse-drawn sleigh and carolers slid out. Inside, there was a round-trip ticket to Vermont, a printout of a car reservation in Vermont for Christmas morning, an address, and a key. He held his breath as his heart raced.

She couldn't have...

She wouldn't...

The idea was too large to think of in one piece. Could she have found his family? Delilah, with her quick fingers and her seemingly endless list of resources. Even if he asked her not to look, wouldn't she? Always prying. Always hunting for answers. That was Delilah...

He took a deep breath.

No, he'd said he didn't want to know them, and she would have known that he meant it. So... He turned the key over in his hand. An airplane ticket, a car, and a house key. Invitation or threat? Or... challenge. She was going to drag him kicking and screaming out of Chicago after all. At least for a few days. He checked the dates on the flight again. There was no way he was going to sleep tonight, and maybe if he arrived early the airline could bump him up to an earlier flight. It was worth a shot.

CHAPTER TWENTY-ONE

Miss Samson,

I owe you. Come to Toronto if you ever want to collect.

—I

THE CAR SWERVED DANGEROUSLY on the icy road. Alan fought the wheel and managed to bring the rental car to a stop next to a snowdrift. Flat tire. It figured. Heavy snowstorms had threatened to close O'Hare airport overnight, so he'd flown out early, not wanting to risk getting snowed in and missing Delilah. But every step since then had been fraught with trouble. The rental agency didn't have cars. When he was finally given a tiny, blue two-door POS, the onboard GPS couldn't find the highway he needed. Then the GPS talked in Swedish for five miles. And now there was a flat tire.

Movement out of the corner of his eye made Alan turn. The little red sedan that had followed him since town had stopped behind him and the single occupant, a blonde woman wearing a sweater and jeans, was picking her way through the snow to him. She was thirty, maybe a few years older. Alan rolled down the window. "I'm fine. You can keep going."

"And how are you going to get anywhere with a flat tire?" the woman asked. Fine lines appeared around her eyes when she smiled and he bumped his estimation of her age up an extra ten years.

"I'll be fine. I can call the rental company. Get a tow truck." Be late. Hopefully Delilah would forgive him.

"Do you have cell reception?" the woman asked.

Alan pulled out his phone to check. No signal.

His face must have given her the answer. "Why don't you come with me?" she asked. "Our cabin's five miles from here, and we have a land line."

"I don't know if I should leave the car," Alan said. "My girlfriend—uh, friend..."—my something—"paid for it. I don't want her to get in trouble."

"I hate to break it to you, kiddo, but no one's going to steal that car. People in rural Vermont aren't that desperate for bad transportation."

He smiled. "Yeah, I don't even know why it was on the rental lot."

"This girlfriend's breaking up with you?" the woman guessed.

"I hope not. They told me they had someone break into the lot last night. All the fences were broken. This is probably the rental agent's car." And he'd given it a flat tire driving on the icy, bumpy, rural road.

"Pop the trunk," the woman said. "I'll take you to my place and you can call from there. Come on. I don't bite!"

Alan felt the blood rush to his cheeks. "Thanks, um. Miss?"

"Missus," she said as he climbed out of the car, "but I'll take the compliment. You can call me Tabitha."

He grabbed his carry-on bag out of the trunk, locked the little car, and climbed into the tropical warmth of Tabitha's car. "So, you're not a native New Englander?"

She laughed. "Is it that obvious? Actually, I was born as far away from New England as you can get on the East Coast. Born and raised in Coral Gables, outside Miami. Beautiful place. I hate it."

"Um? That's a little..."

"Harsh?" Tabitha waved a hand. "It was miserable. My parents ignored me and even paradise gets lonely. But that's old news. I got married just after college, had five babies who are all grown up, and life is pretty darn perfect now."

Alan laughed. "Wow. Um, okay. I don't know what to say, sorry. I'm not a family person, I guess."

"Only child?" Tabitha asked as they wound through the scenic pine forest.

"Foster child. No one wanted me." Except Delilah. Maybe. He drummed his fingers on his knee.

Tabitha leaned forward, blue eyes sparkling. "So, this is me being a nosy future grandma, but are you ever going to be a family person? Is this girlfriend The One? Are you going to settle down?" She waited a beat and asked, "Are you going to run screaming because I'm asking?"

"Are all potential mother-in-laws like you?"

Tabitha's smile split into a cheery grin. "Of course not! You don't meet a girl like me every dynasty." When he didn't respond quickly enough she nudged him with her elbow. "You need to brush up on your Disney references." The car turned down a street lined with feathery pine boughs that bent under heavy snow to form a dreamlike tunnel. "Ah, there we are. Home sweet holiday rental home. I wanted to stay in Texas, but my second daughter got to pick the location for Christmas this year and she decided we needed a rustic retreat. Or so she says. I think it's because Major Cobb's family lives nearby."

"Who?" Alan asked as the car pulled to a stop outside a stone mansion that could only be considered rustic by someone who thought Chicago was a cute little town. Delilah would have loved it.

"Major Cobb? He was our neighbor years and years ago. My youngest daughter has been engaged to his oldest son since kindergarten. She's usually in

Africa, my youngest daughter that is, so getting her to leave work for a week was like pulling teeth. We bribed her with having the Cobbs nearby."

Alan followed her inside to a cozy living room with a roaring fire and a towering, undecorated, Christmas tree. "Did you guys just get here?"

"Last night," Tabitha said. "Here, make yourself comfy. I bet there's cookies baking."

"Isn't it dangerous to leave the stove on while no one's home?"

Tabitha tilted her head in confusion. "Oh. Yes. It would be. But there's always someone at home. We don't have minions for nothing!" Her eyes widened. "I meant kids. Not minions. I don't have real minions. Who would? That's a super villain-ish thing, and I'm obviously not a villain. Or a super-human. Or anything. And if I were, I would totally be a superhero with a very cute outfit. But there are kids here. My son and baby-son-in-law and my extra-son are downstairs playing video games. One's natural birth, one we had by marriage, and the other we had by adoption at gun point."

The clock ticked loudly as he stared.

Tabitha frowned. "Sorry. Is that over-sharing?"

"No, no, it's just, I..." He almost said he knew a family with minions, but that way led to awkward-ness and more stunned silences. Tabitha would probably think he had a concussion. Normal people did not take genetically engineered minions for granted. "Sorry. Why..." He shook his head. "I don't know how to frame this question."

"I look so normal, so why am I not a member of the two-point-five WPF club?"

He nodded uncomfortably.

She grinned. "Because two-point-five kids is very hard to arrange for, I always wanted a big family, and white picket fences don't go with castles."

Alan dropped his bag on the kitchen table. "Castle? Did you say castle?"

"It's just a little one," Tabitha said as she checked the oven for cookies. "In retrospect, I shouldn't have told my husband to have a house picked out by the time I left the hospital with our youngest. But I didn't want to go home to the house he'd set on fire—"

"Fire?" Alan shook his head again, wondering if he'd heard correctly. "You're joking, right?"

Tabitha pulled a tray from the oven and flipped cookies off with a spatula, shaking her head. "Oh, no. Evan's a wonderful man, practically perfect, but he doesn't cook very well. He gets distracted, and it turns out grilled cheese is flammable. No one was hurt, but I did let him do the house hunting while I was in the hospital with complications."

"Buying a castle seems a little extravagant."

"Oh, no, he got it for a steal." She brought the cookies over. "Have a seat, you're not in a rush are you?"

"I should call the rental company and get out of your hair," Alan said, reeling a little.

Tabitha waved his suggestion away. "Nonsense. You look like a young man who's had too much stress and not enough food lately. Eat a cookie and tell me about this girl of yours."

"She's not mine," Alan said reluctantly as he sat down. "We're kind of complicated at the moment."

Tabitha smiled, a warm, genuine expression that wrapped around him like perfect acceptance. "All relationships are complicated. What's she like?"

Alan bit into his cookie and tried to come up with a good answer. "Amazing? She's so self-assured. Confident. I'm used to working with drama queens and people who melt down over every little thing, and she's always so calm. She's intelligent, beautiful, fun to be with. I can relax with her, joke around..." He trailed off. She was Delilah. How else could he say it?

"Sounds like love," Tabitha said before taking a bite of her own cookie.

"Is it?" Alan asked. "I liked her for ages but she kept turning me down. Sometimes I think it's all a daydream."

Tabitha brushed cookie crumbs off the table, avoiding eye contact. "Why'd she turn you down?"

"Bad first impression. She says I look like a hitman."

She met his gaze at that. "Are you?"

Alan raised his eyebrows. "What sort of question is that?"

"An obvious one," Tabitha said. "You aren't from Wyoming, are you? Because it would be really funny if you were."

"Because you know a hitman in Wyoming?" Alan gues-sed. "No. I'm from Illinois and I'm in politics. Local, not national."

Tabitha sighed. "Well, I suppose a reunion was too much to hope for."

"How does that tie in with hitman?"

"I knew one, back in the day. He's dead now. Punched his pregnant girlfriend and a passerby broke his head on the concrete for it. The son's much nicer from what I hear. Lives up in Wyoming with his grandparents. I always wondered if he'd follow in his father's footsteps." She shrugged. "Do you want another cookie?"

"That's not a normal segue."

This time her grin was impish as she waggled her eyebrows at him. "It is in this house."

Alan leaned back in his chair and watched as Tabitha plated more cookies and poured milk. "You look very familiar."

"I get that a lot," she said. "If I was wearing a white sweater you'd get it right away. It's become something of a signature color for me."

He tried picturing her in white and the image fixed in his mind. "Zephyr Girl."

Milk sprayed across the table as she coughed. "Excuse me?"

"Zephyr Girl. You look like Zephyr Girl." Killed in a fight with Doctor Charm according to rumors. Although, since he'd had lunch with Doctor Charm, maybe Zephyr Girl was still flying around somewhere. Hard to picture a superhero baking cookies though.

Tabitha's eyebrows bounced skyward. "Really? I usually get Pacifica from *Fractured*. The TV show." She paused. "You've never seen it? My oldest daughter played the superhero Pacifica on the TV show and she looks just like me. Younger, of course, and a bit firmer all around. But that's age for you."

He shelved the budding daydream of meeting a childhood hero. "Sorry, I'm not familiar with the show." Watching TV took time that he could never seem to squeeze into the day. Especially once he'd started chasing after Delilah.

"Really? It's popular with the superhero-believer set."

Alan shrugged. "I'm not sure I believe in heroes, super powered or otherwise. People are just people. They make good choices. They make bad choices. At the end of the day all you can hope is that you did more good than harm."

An alarming grumble shook the house and Tabitha sat up, eyes bright. "What's that?" Alan asked.

"The garage door. The conquerors have returned. I hope they remembered the onions for the soup."

He cleaned up his seat at the table. "I'll go step outside and call the tow truck. Happy holidays."

"What?" Tabitha frowned at him. "There's no need to rush off. Sit down and try to act suitably rescued. If I start dragging eligible bachelors home, I'll be accused of having Mrs. Bennet Syndrome. This needs to look completely accidental."

"It was accidental." He laughed. "You couldn't give me a flat tire!"

She didn't laugh along.

Suddenly the kitchen air was too thick to breath. The whole conversation had been slightly to the left of normal, and now Alan wondered if he hadn't wandered into much more dangerous territory. Maybe Tabitha was an ax murderer. Maybe the onions were for fresh politician soup.

"Mom!" a young man's voice shouted from the basement. "Mom, Blessing threw me in the snow!"

Tabitha smiled. "Aren't kids adorable?"

"I... Uh..."

"Mom?" A far more familiar voice said as light footfalls ran up the stairs. Delilah turned the corner into the kitchen and halted. "Alan."

"D-Delilah. Hi. I... Uh... I just... My car got a flat tire." He forced his hands to stop moving.

She tilted her head—just like her mother. He knew he'd seen that gesture before! "You're not supposed to be here for another six hours!"

"I got an early flight ahead of the snowstorm."

"I had a red sweater all picked out!" Delilah cried. "I don't even have make-up on!"

He swallowed. "You... You look great." And hopefully she hadn't heard the raw desire she'd inspired in his voice.

"He's right," Tabitha added. "You look amazing without makeup. You're father's genes, I think. No one in my family has eyelashes like that."

Delilah turned on her mother. "What is he doing here?"

"Sweetheart?" Doctor Charm turned the corner, hands full of groceries.

Alan's shoulder blades hit the wall behind him. But it was far too late. The whole family was crowding into the kitchen to see what was going on. A blonde woman who could only be Tabitha's oldest daughter was holding hands with someone who resembled Arktos from L.A. too closely for it to be coincidence. Travys was in the back with two other young men, one who looked like Delilah and the other like Arktos, along with two other women Alan assu-med were Delilah's other sisters.

He panicked and slipped into the shadows.

What had he been thinking? Big family holiday? Had he lost his mind? Families had to start small! You added one person at a time! You didn't just pick up the deluxe edition wholesale one afternoon.

The chill of the outside brought Alan back to his senses and he leaned against a pine tree for support.

"Alan?" Delilah's voice echoed across the yard. "Alan?" She ran to him, scarf trailing behind her. "What's wrong?"

He stared at her.

"Alan?" She stopped a few feet away. "Are you okay?"

"I wasn't expecting the whole herd at once."

She glanced over her shoulder at the house. "Yeah, I meant to break them to you slowly. I did say I had a big family."

"You didn't tell me that's what was waiting in Ver-mont!"

Delilah shrugged. "You said you wanted a big family holiday. This is the only family I have." She caught his hand. "Come on. Come inside and meet them. Once you get to know them, they aren't so scary."

"Your mother is Zephyr Girl and she told me over cookies about how a hit man she knew got killed!"

"But she left out the part about how she's the one that killed him. That's progress."

"That's scary."

Delilah leaned in close, pressing herself against him. "It could be worse?"

"How?"

"They could all be normals."

He let that sink in. Then he raised an eyebrow. "They're all superheroes?"

"Mostly villains, but a few of them are heroes." She wrapped her arms around him. "Come on, isn't this better? They all know how you feel. They all know what it's like to not be like everyone else. You'll have someone to sit with and discuss chasing criminals, or having a secret identity. How many in-laws could you do that with?"

Alan held her tightly. "And what happens if they don't like me?"

"Why wouldn't they like you?" She squeezed him. "You aren't six any more. No one is taking you away from me. If this is too much, we can go do Christmas by ourselves somewhere else. We can find a hotel, or fly back to Chicago."

Visions of Christmas alone flashed through his mind, followed by images of what he and Delilah could get up to alone. He swallowed again. But... She'd brought him to meet the family. That had to count for something, didn't it? "We can stay," he said at last. "I want to meet your family. Really. I just wasn't prepared for this. Flat tires don't usually lead to your future mother-in-law interrogating you."

"Mother-in-law?" Delilah laughed. "Aren't we skipping a few steps?"

He blushed. "Potential mother-in-law. Mother of the woman I am dating. You know what I mean."

She kissed him gently. "Come back inside and I promise not to tease you about that slip up too much."

He took her hand, holding it just a little more tightly that he should have. "Okay," he said. "Okay."

CHAPTER TWENTY-TWO

To: Delilah
With Love: Alan

DELILAH CURLED HER LEGS up on the big comfy chair and watched Alan ease into the deep waters of Smith family living. He'd lost the deer-in-the-headlights look over dinner and was playing video games with the younger boys. Now all he had to do was defrost enough to talk to her sisters.

Maria collapsed in the sofa beside her. "Do you know how hard it is to lose an election?"

"Apropos of nothing," Delilah murmured toying with the necklace Alan had given her for Christmas. "No. Is that where you've been?"

"Yes! And it's not going well."

"Does it concern a certain superhero who thinks he's a god?"

Maria scowled at the ceiling. "I'm not answering that."

"You like him."

Her sister glared. "So what? At least I'm not engaged to a boy scout! He's so squeaky clean he makes my teeth hurt."

Delilah watched Alan, who was talking with Ty about something involving hand gestures. He noticed her staring and smiled. Delilah smiled back. "I like him. And we're not engaged. We're dating."

"You brought him home," Maria said bluntly. "Let me list the guys who have been introduced to the family: Noah, Tyler, and Alan."

"And Travys and Aaron," she said, adding in their adopted sibling and Tyler's little brother. She sipped her hot cider. "And Martin."

"Dad only met Martin because he had to come post bail for us," Maria said tartly. "It's not the same."

"You would have brought him home eventually."

Maria rolled her eyes and sat up. "Maybe. But I was young and stupid then." She glared at Alan. "Do you really think he's good enough for you?"

"Do you really think he's not?" Delilah challenged her.

Alan stood up and walked over to them, folding his arms over his chest. "Do you really think his hearing's that bad?"

Maria's eyes narrowed. "If you hurt my sister..."

"They'll never find my body," Alan finished for her. "Yes. I think I caught the gist of that threat the first time." He reached down and twined his fingers with Delilah's. "Do you know, you have a very over-protective family, Love. I swear the only person who was excited to see me was your mother."

"He's cute! We should keep him!" Mom chimed from across the room.

Delilah put her cup to the side. "Let's go for a walk."

She pulled Alan away from the festivities and out into the winter darkness. Starlight glittered on the diamond-and-topaz necklace he'd had given her. For him, she'd bought a pair of season tickets to the Bulls games. It didn't meet the agreed twenty-dollar limit, but then again, neither had his. And it wasn't her only present for him, either.

The snow crunched under their boots as they walked away from the house.

"It's beautiful out here." Alan sounded wistful, as if he still wasn't convinced that it was real.

"I thought so." Vermont was picturesque. Not a place she'd want to live permanently, but worth visiting from time to time.

He laced his fingers with hers. "We're not planning on retiring here, are we?"

Delilah laughed. "We?"

"Family Christmas, exchanging gifts, I don't know. I'm feeling a bit we-ish." He looked sideways at her with a smile. "I like being part of a We."

His joy was radiant. She leaned against his shoulder and he moved so she was in front of him, his arms wrapped around her waist, chin resting on her head. After a moment, she reached into her coat pocket and pulled out the thick white-gold ring she'd bought several days before. "What do you think about making the We a permanent thing?"

There was a stillness behind her and she gripped his hands to keep him from running away. A barn owl's distinctive call shattered the deathly silence around them.

"Do I need to get down on one knee?" she added, laughing because it was the only way to keep from crying. If he said no... Well, she wouldn't be a Smith if she didn't have a contingency plan for that kind of disaster. But she'd like not to need it.

Alan took the ring from her. "I don't have one for you."

"We can go shopping when we get home." He was playing with it. Turning the ring around so it caught the moonlight. But he wasn't saying yes.

Delilah's heart pounded.

"Where will we live?"

She shrugged, keeping her voice utterly neutral. "Your house. Mine. Neither. Both. Somewhere in Chicago, but I'm not picky." But she'd appreciate it if he would hurry up and answer, because in a second she'd forget how to breathe.

His gaze flicked up and met hers, and he softened into something much gentler than a smile. "Yes," he said. "I love you."

He slipped the ring on, and Delilah remembered how to breathe. Everything was perfect. She stretched up and kissed him under the winter stars. After all, even villains could have happy endings.

Sharp-eyed viewers spotted some shiny swag on Chicago's newly elected mayor. During the city council press conference, several people noticed that Mayor Adale was sporting a swanky new ring on his left hand. The new mayor later confirmed that he and Delilah Samson of Subrosa Securities had gotten engaged over the winter holidays. Although Chicago's infamous gossip mill has long had the two paired together, this is the first public confirmation of their relationship. The couple plans to marry this spring and hold a public reception for family, friends, and well-wishers at the Chicago Field Museum.

THANK YOU!

Dear Reader,

Thank you for taking the time to read this book. I hope you enjoyed reading it as much as I enjoyed writing it.

The best way to support books you love is to spread the word: word of mouth still sells more books than any other method. If you'd like to see more *Heroes and Villains* books, please consider leaving a review at the outlet where you bought this book.

And of course, don't forget to say hi either on Twitter (@lianabrooks), on Facebook (Liana Brooks), or on my blog (www.lianabrooks.com).

Liana

ABOUT THE AUTHOR

Liana Brooks was born in San Diego, California. Years later she was disappointed to learn that The Shire was not some place she could move to, nor was Rider of Rohan an acceptable career choice. Studying marine biology so she could play with sharks seemed to be the only alternative. After college Liana settled down to work as a full-time author and mother because logical career progression is something that happens to other people. When she grows up, Liana wants to be an Evil Overlord and take over the world.

In the meantime, she writes sci fi and SFR in between trips to the beach. She can be found wearing colorful socks on the Emerald Coast, or online at www.lianabrooks.com.

SNEAK PEEK:
THE POLAR TERROR

CHAPTER ONE

KADDY LEANED HER HEAD against the pale yellow wall of the hospital room, closed her eyes, and tried not to hear the constant whooshing and beeping of the machines.

The ticky-tick-tick of the heartrate monitor.

The two-minute beep as the IV dropped another controlled dose of pain medications that seemed to do no good.

The whock-whock-whock of the second hand on the clock.

There was no escape.

She couldn't even run outside to the snow and let that peace envelope her. Not while Everett was lying in bed, staring out the window at the flat roof of the parking garage, refusing to talk.

With a sigh, she tried to reach him. Again. "Do you want to watch some TV?"

Everett didn't move.

"We could play with your action figures." She pushed herself out of the uncomfortable chair and walked over to his bed.

Everett let her pull the plush Polar Terror doll out of his listless hand.

She bopped him on the nose with it. "The Polar Terror is coming! He'll walk right out of this storm and—"

Everett rolled to the side, crossing his tiny arms as best he could. His bottom lip quavered with anger and pain.

"I'm sorry." Kaddy put the doll back next to him. "We're going to find a way through this, Ev. I promise. And then we'll sew you the Polar Terror costume you wanted."

"There is no Polar Terror," Everett whispered, his first words all day. "Nobody comes to rescue you."

She rubbed his shoulder gently. "I know, bud. That's why you have me. You and me, we can handle anything."

"Not this," he whispered. "Not cancer."

Tears choked her. "We will," she whispered just as a softly. "We'll find a way to make it all right."

Everett squeezed his eyes shut.

Kaddy slumped back. Even if—and it was a really big if—the hospital pulled off a miracle and Everett got better, she wasn't going back to a job.

Her firm had been very patient, let her take a leave of absence, but her boss was retiring and the incoming boss hadn't liked her. He'd questioned her education, her field time, her work ethic… And while the guy couldn't come out and say it, his tone all but screamed SINGLE MOMS NEED NOT APPLY.

She shook her head. Being a single mom hadn't been her choice. She wasn't even dating when Everett was born.

But then there'd been a car accident a semester be-fore graduation. Her sister and brother-in-law were killed on impact.

The idea of being a working, single parent was terrifying, but letting Everett bounce between foster families wasn't an option either.

Squeezing the guard rail of his hospital bed, she stood up. One way or another, she'd make a good life for him. That's what moms did.

There was a tentative knock at the door, like the person on the other side was hoping they wouldn't get an answer, but knew they would.

Rolling her eyes, Kaddy cracked it open for the inevitable nurse.

Andrea, the ever-perky Dream Coordinator for Merriton Pediatric Hospital, looked at her with the world's fakest smile, wide, frightened blue eyes, and damp blonde hair that looked like she'd gone outside without her usual hat.

"Yesssss?" Kaddy dragged the word out.

Andrea squeezed through the tiny crack in the doorway and slammed the door shut. "Okay. Hi, Kaddy! Everett! It is so good to see you two!" The words were rushed, panicked, and had the forced joviality of true terror.

But this was the Yukon in mid-winter, not some American city where a bomber was going to hold them hostage. "Is... is everything okay?" Kaddy asked.

The only thing that would scare Andrea was a really bad diagnosis. Kaddy's stomach flipped as tears welled up in her eyes. She couldn't handle that.

"Just dandy!" Andrea's voice squeaked. "Actually." She faked a laugh. "Funny story. Everett has a visitor. And, I know he's been so tuckered out, the poor thing, so I was thinking we should reschedule. Don't you? That's great!" she rushed on, not letting Kaddy answer. "I'll cancel. He can come back some other time."

Not bad news then.

Everett rolled over in his bed, forehead wrinkled in confusion.

"Who came?" Kaddy asked. The hospital attracted an eclectic group of visitors. Usually hockey stars, medical students, and politicians on goodwill tours. But Andrea welcomed all of them with open arms. "It isn't the Maple Leafs again, is it?" No one this far north loved the Maple Leafs.

Andrea's head shook so hard Kaddy worried the woman was going to give herself a concussion.

"Okay..." Kaddy glanced over at Everett who was showing the first interest in anything since his chemo treatment two days earlier. "Is there a reason you don't want this person to see Everett?" She licked her lips and mouthed, *Is it child services?*

"Worse," Andrea whispered hoarsely. She leaned forward and murmured a name in Kaddy's ear.

Kaddy's eyebrows went up in surprise. "Like… for real? You—" She stopped herself just in time and leaned forward. "You found a cosplayer to play the Polar Terror?"

She couldn't keep the excitement out of her whisper. Everett was going to be over the moon.

"No." Andrea shook her head and glanced over her shoulder. The color drained from her face. "He's… he's not fake."

"Who isn't fake?" Everett demanded from the bed.

"Just say no." Andrea grabbed Kaddy's elbow. "Please?"

Kaddy shook the other woman off and looked at the door. There was a thin layer of frost on the door. A suspiciously thin layer. Like someone was intentionally cooling the door for a grand entrance.

She narrowed her eyes.

Would the Dream Coordinator come in here acting terrified just to sell the idea of a super villain at the hospital? Yes. Yes she would.

It's exactly the sort of thing a perky, cheerful-before-coffee, former cheerleader would do.

Kaddy crossed her arms and sighed dramatically. "I don't know, Andrea. Ev's had a really rough week.

I don't think he should have visitors. Not even the Polar Terror."

The heartrate monitor screamed in excitement as Everett sat up like he was attached to a spring. "The Polar Terror?"

With a burst of cold air, the door fell inward. Ice crystals glittered as icicles formed on the ceiling.

That was some impressive special effects budget.

A man in the Polar Terror's costume stepped in, towering over even Kaddy, who hadn't been called short since she turned thirteen and shot up. The muskrat parka, a rabbit fur hat, a strip of seal skin, a fur pouch, beadwork on his boots… and of course the very modern black balaclava with the Under Armor logo.

The Polar Terror had come to Merriton.

Head to
www.inkprintpress.com/lianabrooks/
heroesandvillains/polarterror/
to keep reading today!